Touched Out

By Robert McCutcheon

Bellissima Publishing, LLC
Jamul, California
www.bellissimapublishing.com

IBSN 1-935118-30-7
First Edition

Touched Out

By Robert McCutcheon

Sometimes you can't see the forest because of the trees.

CHAPTER ONE

Missing Brothers

"What are you doing?"

"What does it look like I'm doing?"

"I'd rather not speculate."

In what two seconds before had been the post-school solitude of a standard suburban kitchen, Teddy Livingstone had placidly been pouring Coca-Cola into a translucent blue ice-cube tray, one of four that their freezer contained at any given time. As always, however, the open door of the refrigerator had caused a crowd to form, a crowd consisting on this occasion of his older brother, Billy.

"What I'm doing," I said, "is for everyone's benefit. I'm making Coke ice cubes."

"I don't mean to sound ungrateful," Billy said, "but I like to be able to swallow my beverages."

"Well, now, see, moron?" I answered. "I'm about to improve your standard of living. Now you'll be able to use these ice cubes instead of regular ones when you fix a glass of Coke."

His point made, Teddy momentarily regretted calling his brother a moron. In truth, he wasn't sure in what mood he should be. It was not yet three o'clock, and school had not yet been back in session a full week. Outside, the sun was blazing in a clear blue sky. White clouds snapped in the breeze like sheets on a line. He had hiked up the hill from the bus stop with Hooty and some other friends; two guys had taken their shirts off en route. Now the gaps in the kitchen windows above the curtains glowed like ingots of light. About this time the pool should have been thrashing with kids just before the guard's whistle announcing the mid-afternoon adult swim (except that the pool had been drained the day after Labor Day, turning their suburb into an asphalt desert).

"And?" Billy asked.

"When they melt, the Coke in the glass won't get watered down."

"Well, the Coke will still get flat when the ice cubes melt, won't it? I mean, the frozen Coke won't keep its carbonation, will it? Maybe the Coke won't be watered down, but it will be gassed down, so to speak."

As his brother offered these comments, Teddy was sighting along the top of the tray, trying to keep the liquid it contained from spilling from one compartment into another. Occasionally, he liked to flood a tray creating a pane of ice above and cubes below in a sort of candy-bar effect; but the fact that this tray might have a head complicated the whole procedure.

"I think you'll be disappointed in the texture of the ice cubes, also," Billy said.

As soon as the surface of the Coca-Cola in the ice cube tray had calmed, Teddy was free to wheel on his brother the industrial chemist.

"You know what you are?" I asked. "You're a negative."

"I'll take that as a compliment."

Billy shouldered by Teddy to the refrigerator. He opened the door and reached for the stoppered sixteen-ounce bottle, which counter to Teddy's calculations still showed a pretty good cuff of Coke, a good four ounces (whereas it was family policy to leave no more than a molecular level of liquid on the bottom of the bottle for the next drinker, just enough to give the glass some color).

"You'll ruin a perfectly good insult," I said.

"We just did a unit on negative numbers in math class," Billy said after a swig from the bottle. "They have some interesting properties, more interesting in some ways than positive numbers."

When Teddy had called his brother a moron he hadn't been thinking in academic terms. Billy was taking a special, advanced class for the three or four seniors who had exhausted all the math courses the high school had to offer, including calculus. Once on a hall pass Teddy looked through the window in their classroom door and saw them in action. The teacher's desk was empty. He and the students circled a few of the small desks by a blackboard in one corner of the room. (They ate lunch during class.)

Teddy not called his brother "negative" with much conviction either. He'd just learned the word (at least in that sense) earlier the same day in English class. Their teacher used it to describe certain characters in a novel they were reading who didn't particularly resemble Billy, or for that matter any other people Teddy had ever encountered, although (of course) he had not yet been a ship chandler in the Dutch East Indies.

"What does Teddy Livingstone think of that?"

On cue, Mrs. Livingstone entered the kitchen. She walked straight up to her youngest son, glowering over the girlish fist that she held up to her face. Teddy instinctively flattened himself against the refrigerator under this fresh assault. Closer inspection, however, revealed his mother's grimace to be the product of suppressed laughter.

"What word would Teddy Livingstone use to describe *himself?*" she asked into her fist. "Positive? Negative?"

"Zero?" Billy chimed in questioning Teddy.

Obviously, Mrs. Livingstone had launched into one of her routines, and Billy had stepped forward to play straight man. Recognizing their numerical advantage, Teddy let his arms drop to his sides. His shoulders suddenly ached, as though his hanging hands held the suitcases of resignation.

It was probably too early to check on the ice cubes.

"Don't those talk show hosts drive you crazy?" Mom then asked in her normal voice. "They think they're so clever when they phrase their questions in the third person. 'What is Arthur Godfrey's greatest fear?' Honestly!"

Although he both endorsed and practiced the technique, Teddy shook his head in commiseration with his mother. At least until she shot her right hand, which a minute before had simulated a microphone, into the air and waved, back in character.

"Well, I can't stay," she said. "I know you'll understand."

Billy and I exchanged a glance. She had lost him, too.

Her wave turned into a flourish of dismissal as she proffered, "Oh, those guests don't have anywhere to go. They have to make themselves seem in demand. Really! They just don't want to have to sit through a commercial. But I do. I have a date with some dirty clothes," she added. Before she closed the door to the basement behind her, she looked back and said, "You boys miss your brother."

She closed the door and clattered down the wooden steps to the laundry room. A minute later the house shuddered around us as the washing machine lurched into motion.

"Do you really think I'm a negative?" Billy asked.

CHAPTER TWO

The Empty Room

The day we all embarked in a loaded station wagon to drop Chip off at his dorm didn't seem much like the start of a school year. It seemed more like a summer vacation. The University of Pittsburgh started early, before Labor Day; and freshmen had to report for orientation a week before that. The route was familiar. We had driven into Oakland as a family countless times for several dubious cultural events that ranged from concerts to flower shows. On the way there we passed our church, already stony and silent early on this sweltering Sunday afternoon. In Oakland we found a parking space right on Fifth Avenue. While Mom set off on foot to look for an open drug store where she could buy a soap dish for Chip, the men of the family joined the procession of parents and kids hauling boxes and suitcases along the sidewalk. Just in front of us a guy was pulling his son's trunk out of a plumber's panel truck.

Chip's dorm was one of three cylindrical high-rise buildings between Fifth and Forbes. After a trip up two flights of stairs—there were lines at both elevators—we found Chip's roommate already installed, propped up on the bed by the door in khaki slacks and a short-sleeved dress shirt, reading. He looked ready for his first exam. His name was Chip too, but it was short for Chester rather than Charles. He was from New Rochelle, New York. We missed his parents by five minutes. The sensation I had that we had arrived at a sea-side resort followed me over to Chip's window where I stuck my head out into a hot, grainy wind and heard surf. Then I realized that the sound was coming from Forbes Field. It was the cheering of a crowd. The Pirates were playing that day.

The night before, Chip had called Billy and me into his room. We sat on his bed slouching against opposite walls as he told us one of us should move into his room after he left. We could decide who. He wouldn't be back much during the school year, and he didn't know whether he would take his summer job at the pool again or if he would even stay in Pittsburgh. When he came home for visits he said he could always sleep in the game room.

He was back the following weekend. Freshman orientation was over. Registration was on Monday. When Mom and Dad organized a big family cookout in his honor that Saturday night I felt that perhaps I should remind them that he hadn't graduated yet, and he'd only been gone four days. Billy and I continued to share our room.

I suppose my mother was right. I must have missed Chip. I was certainly aware of his absence in all kinds of ways. Some of them were welcome. My mixed feelings, like most of my feelings, were most intense in the kitchen. Once Chip left, when I was the first person to enter that room on a weekend morning, Chip wouldn't already be sitting there at the table having a leisurely, well-deserved, post-workout breakfast. I enjoyed having the kitchen to myself, but I missed the remains of Chip's meals. He was famous for eating three-quarters of a piece of fruit. He would carefully slice several pieces from the item with the appropriate knife and leave a disk of apple or an apostrophe of banana behind. (In the fruit drawer of the refrigerator you might come across a half-grapefruit with four sections remaining.) No one knew the cause of Chip's habit. As far as I knew, no one had ever asked. Perhaps he wanted always to be prepared with visual aids on the order of pie graphs if he was called on to give a presentation to an unscheduled breakfast meeting. I often made my own meal of Chip's leftovers, a practice that over the years had earned me the title of 'one-man clean-up crew' from him. Now, confronted with a bowl of fruit, globular and intact, I hardly knew where to begin. It seemed presumptuous of me to take the first bite of anything, ever! And since the refrigerator no longer routinely contained anything partially consumed and/or in the early stages of decay, I couldn't as easily portray my constant foraging as a public service.

With Chip gone there was no reason to have fried chicken every Friday night. We had it anyway.

Even though all the evidence of my eldest brother was missing, I often sensed him in the kitchen watching. Sometimes I suspected that he hadn't left home at all, but he had instead expanded all of a sudden into a different dimension. He wasn't gone, he was just too big to see. He contained us. We didn't notice him for the same reason that on a map you sometimes can't make out the name of the country at which you are looking because the letters are too widely spaced. I had long held the theory that our solar system was just an atom in the molecule of the galaxy and that conversely every molecule in our body contained innumerable solar systems. Chip just moved up one order of magnitude. He shot out in every direction from his center and ours. Logically, that made him a kind of Orion and the rest of the family inhabitants of his belt. But more often I had the sensation of his face superimposed on the kitchen. The countertops became a warm, Formica smile. The more alone I was, the more observed I felt.

After Chip left—physically, anyway—my relationship with

my other brother (never a textbook example of normality) veered still farther into the deviant. Instead of standing on his sudden seniority, Billy became deferential in all kinds of unforeseeable ways. Not only did he *not* take over Chip's room, which despite its single bed was slightly larger than ours, he urged me to take it. He formed the concept of "privacy." (He knocked before he entered our room.)

"I know I snore," he said to me one day, although he gave no indication that he was aware that when he wasn't snoring he was conducting seminars with himself in his sleep.

This reaction to Chip's departure reminded me of an earlier phase in our career as brothers, a few years earlier, when Billy hit puberty. Or maybe it was vice versa. Through no fault of his own, Billy began to germinate. He grew several inches a day, wrists first. His voice dropped two octaves overnight and acquired the resonance of a drainage pipe. He turned his back when he undressed and clutched a towel around his waist if he had to cover *any* distance naked, *even* in our room. Hormones pulsed visibly through his veins. His skin broke out. From the vantage point of pre-adolescence, it was like sleeping next to a Petri dish.

Billy could be as furtive as he wanted to be in the various locker rooms he frequented; however, he couldn't conceal these developments from me. As far as I knew they were unprecedented.

All Chip's rites of passage took place behind the closed door of his bedroom; and anyway, I had considered him an adult all my life. You would think that my roommate's acquisitions might awe me into submission, but just the opposite transpired. Billy became docility personified. Due to the fact that with every step he was likely to knock over some object with his outsized limbs, he wouldn't make a move without orders from me. A slick, hairless stick figure, I jabbed a finger at him and barked commands as he stooped along beside me. You might have thought he was always in the act of inhaling, but not really. He was just trying his best to shrink to his former dimensions and to suck his body hair back into his skin! This state of affairs persisted until I followed Billy into the halls of manhood, and then it was like that all over again!

Although I didn't sleep there, I occasionally studied in Chip's room. I already knew its contents by heart, down to the pellet gun leaning against the pillar of old Playboys stacked on the floor, not camouflaged, in a corner of the closet. As a class, athlete swimmers don't accumulate much equipment—maybe a tank suit hanging on the back of a chair or a stray kickboard. However, Chip occasionally played other sports; and his closet door opened with a musty whiff of leather and pigskin.

By now the titles of all the paperbacks shelved on the carpet along the baseboards of the room were familiar to me, from current novels to classics, a category that according to our high school curriculum included any book that had been condensed either in a comic book or Reader's Digest. When we knew he would be out for a while, Hooty and I used to play a game in Chip's room. We would each pick one of the newer, thicker paperbacks and see who could find a dirty part first. I was rarely bested. The key was to look in the middle third of the book, toward the end of a chapter or section. That is, you wouldn't begin at the front of the book, since I had yet to find the novel so filthy as to open with a sex scene; and by the end of a book, its characters' passions have cooled, and they have to figure out how remorseful to be. You had to look for a gap between paragraphs in the middle of the book and backtrack from there. Hooty never seemed to catch on to this.

There were also a few coffee-table books in Chip's room, although there was no coffee table on which to put them. He had a couple of volumes of Life photography, and the family copy of the New Yorker carton album found its way into his room and stayed there. You could look at this book as the extreme soft end of soft-core pornography. The 'forties' section displayed some very buxom Betty Grable types, some nude, for which I had developed a taste. Bobbed hair seemed to be in and nipples out of fashion. I browsed through the cartoons on a different principle, trying to avoid the good parts and discover cartoons I hadn't before noticed. Every few pages I would run across one of Chip's favorites and adopt it as my own. One showed a penguin standing around in a group of fellow birds on an ice floe in a sport coat and ascot, holding a cigarette in one hand and a drink in the other hand. He was saying to another penguin, "I just got damned sick and tired of being formal all the time." Chip seemed to like the World War II-vintage cartoons best, with or without bobbysoxers. In one, a Japanese drill instructor, pointing to phrases on a blackboard, was teaching a classroom full of soldiers how to infiltrate American troops: "Hello, Joe. This are Mike. Please to put down gun and step into open space." Another showed Hitler addressing a crowd with the words, "And I think I can say without fear of contradiction . . . " It was easier for me to laugh when Chip pointed them out to me because I found them genuinely funny. In our less prurient moods Hooty and I played a game where we read captions to each other and had to describe the corresponding cartoons.

Once in a while, absently, I would look up from one book or another at the ribbons pinned to the bulletin board in front of me and forget that they weren't mine. Again I felt observed, this time by a cheering crowd. I felt I should get up from my seat and take a bow. That was usually about the time I realized I had been talking to myself or to Chip.

One night Teddy was sitting at Chip's desk doing homework

for his advanced placement American history course. Suddenly, to his left and slightly behind him, the door swung open, the way they do in saloons in Westerns. T. C., their cat, swaggered into the room. Neither breaking stride nor averting her stare, she walked over and jumped on Chip's bed and from there stepped onto his desk. Stiff-legged, tail tensed, she did a lap around the top of the desk. Then she lay down across Ted's open book and basked in the light of the lamp.

Teddy was sick of studying, anyway. Every history class he had ever taken had the same drawback: they all started at the beginning. For the tenth time in the course of his schooling he was learning that indigo was a major export of the colonial South. No one had ever explained to him what indigo was or why, if it was once so vital to the American economy, it could not presently be purchased in stores.

Within minutes, before his very eyes, T. C. began her parade of multiple personalities. In profile her eye narrowed, her sidelong grin grew still more sly. Languorously at first, she stretched one arm under Teddy's propped-up book. When she met the resistance of (of all things) a pencil, her face filled with indignation and then alarm; and she began to paw frantically at the foreign object. Next, she peered over the side of the desk and still reclining, tried to pry open the drawer. No course of action was left to Teddy but to reach awkwardly under the desk so that he could stick his pencil up over the other side so T. C. could play with it. Five minutes later she was comatose, draped back over Teddy's book.

That night (and every night thereafter) she followed Teddy back to his room. As soon as he got into bed, T. C. wedged herself behind the crook of his knees and fell asleep. Teddy routinely woke up a split second before he fell onto the floor, twisted into the shape of the letter G, while T. C. slept soundly in the geometric center of the bed.

CHAPTER THREE

Big Man on Campus

From the day that Chip left home, conversation at the Livingstone's dinner table was dominated by a single topic: Teddy's projected trip down to Oakland to visit his brother on campus. Teddy himself felt no urgency in the matter. By his calculation, he had two years to carry out this scheme; that is, he would leave for college himself only after Chip's sophomore year at Pitt. And, anyway, Billy should go first.

"Of course, it won't have the same impact for Billy as it will have for you," Mrs. Livingstone said.

"Billy's plans are set," Mr. Livingstone added. "Or, if they're not set by now . . . ." He broke off with a broad smile in Billy's direction.

"I've been down there a million times," Billy announced, not exactly filling in the gap left by his father.

Almost every day Billy got a plump manila envelope in the mail containing another college catalog. They came from all over. There were colleges everywhere. There were some in Maine.

Phlegmatic as he proved to be on the subject of his upcoming campus visit, Ted could not help but be impressed by the scope of the plan when it finally unfolded. In a series of calls to the principal of the high school, Mrs. Livingstone arranged for Teddy to take a half-day off from school so that he could attend a couple of classes at Pitt with Chip. The following day Teddy would report to his classmates on college life.

Mrs. Livingstone saw Ted off at noon on a Thursday from the doorstep of their house as though he were leaving for college himself. He only wished he had a suitcase to carry up the sidewalk to the station wagon parked on the cinder shoulder of the road. Behind his mother, the open front door framed a scene that belonged on a sampler. For the first time Teddy could remember, and just as he was leaving it, their house was effortlessly itself. The living room had the milky glow of electric light diluted by sunlight. Directly in front of the picture window, an armchair upholstered in a bronze-colored fabric smoldered, with dust for smoke. In truth, Teddy couldn't be sure whether the lamps were on or not. Their cat sat as though carved on an arm of the couch. From the front step Teddy could see straight through to the kitchen where, unless he was very much mistaken, the makings of a pot roast lay out on the counter. It was a forbidden view. He should have been in school. He shouldn't know what went on in this silent street on a weekday any more than he should in their church. Or rather, he suddenly felt as though he was seeing his home motionless, like a memory, for the last time.

With as jaunty a wave as he could manage with a mystical vision in progress, he set off in their station wagon to see his brother.

As I drove into Oakland on that bright Thursday, I couldn't see that just because the school year was well under way, it wasn't still summertime. The early afternoon sky was a deep blue, blurred at the horizon with heat. The cars ahead of me on the bypass heading west were chromed with sunlight, and under the Highland Park Bridge the Allegheny River had the dull shine of sheet metal. Water spun over the dam like a roll of aluminum foil. In either direction (until they folded out of sight) the banks of the river were green and glossy with foliage. On the far side of the bridge, along Washington Boulevard, I passed (unchallenged) the state police barracks where I had somehow gotten my driver's license on the first try during the summer. With the windows down, I bathed in the warm air, balmy with the exhaust from the cars of my fellow motorists. I didn't think to turn on the radio until Washington

Boulevard became Fifth Avenue at Penn.

Teddy had always loved the approach to the university. Along Fifth Avenue the houses got progressively bigger, until they were cubes with windows and pillars. At some point (probably when they had pillars but no windows) they stopped being houses and became halls, synagogues, and institutes set down on green squares of lawn. Oakland was like a squat downtown. In another couple of miles the office buildings of Pittsburgh would line Fifth Avenue like shade trees. Teddy had planned all along to park on Ellsworth Avenue where there were no meters and walk the several blocks to the university. He felt invisibly adult among the pedestrians until he glanced in a shop window and remembered he had on a coat and tie, which had the opposite of the intended effect. Mannerly was the last thing he wanted to appear. Chip was waiting for him at the Fifth Avenue entrance of the Cathedral of Learning, the gothic skyscraper at the center of Pitt's campus. A fraternal handshake was out of the question, since Chip held a coke in one hand and books in the other.

It didn't take me long (once I met Chip) to grasp the basic principle of college life: nobody made you do anything. I just didn't see how I was going to convey this sensation of freedom to my classmates the next day as they sat facing me, clamped in the plastic calipers our high school disguised as desks. Nothing I saw around me suggested school as I knew it. Chip led me through a revolving door into the lobby of the Cathedral of Learning, which (as advertized) was church-like. The room was high-ceilinged, dim and solemn, except that at the tables under the arches students lounged around in shorts and tee shirts. A few people sat in front of open books, writing blissfully as whispers ricocheted off the wall beside them.

I followed Chip through the lobby and down some slick stone steps into the basement. There were lockers along the walls. That was reassuring. Over a couple of cokes in the snack bar, Chip showed me his notebook, which contained no notes to speak of but several syllabuses. Classes could apparently meet at any time of the day or night, including Saturdays. You got homework by the week rather than by the day. Tests were scheduled every couple of weeks, in advance, like TV specials. Chip hadn't been to any classes yet that day; but he had two in the afternoon, a history class at two o'clock and a biology lab at three-thirty.

"The lab will be a problem when swimming season starts," he said; "but at least it's just one day a week."

No one seemed to notice that I was crashing Chip's history class. It helped that my sport coat was rolled up on the floor beside my seat impersonating a pile of books. The class met upstairs. (I wondered who would believe me when I told them you took an elevator to class.) It was in a room a little too big for it, a small lecture hall, really, with padded seats and a sloping floor like a movie theater. Instead of a screen on the front wall there was an elaborate set of sliding blackboards that must have been operated by a winch. They were erased; but through the smears of chalk you could still make out a couple of faded, frantic-sounding phrases—"unrest" and "nationalism explodes"—probably slogans from a recently disbanded rally.

The teacher ignored the blackboards. He was a square shaped man in a skinny tie. He sat on the edge of a desk in front of the class, dangling his legs over it as the students sprawled in the first few rows. In fact, the teacher didn't seem to have much on his mind that day. He kept a small, apologetic smile on his face that widened slightly at any student comments, most of which came from one tall guy with a thick voice whose favorite expression was, "That's a subjective viewpoint." When everyone else was scribbling in their notebooks, Chip looked over at me and laughed silently.

This class didn't end, it dissolved. No bell was heard, and at some point teacher and students alike stretched, shuffled papers into piles, and stood up to leave Some people drifted out the door. Others formed small groups in the aisles. A few students immediately circled the teacher, who seemed prepared with a series of shrugs to retract the few statements he had made during class. Chip jerked his head toward the door to remind me we still had a lab to attend. We did, however, have time to stop by his dorm and pick up his roommate who was taking the same lab section.

"Hi, Ches," Chip said, preceding me into his room.

His roommate put down the mechanical pencil he was holding and pushed the chair back from his desk. "Hi, Chas," he said.

"Chas?" I said.

"Well, we have to know who we're talking to," Chip said. "We can't both be 'Chip.'"

"Whereas a simple 'Chuck' would have sufficed," I said.

"What am I? A college student or a cub scout?" Chip asked.

The other Chip smiled at me from his seat. I might have been wrong, but it seemed to me he was wearing the exact same clothes he wore the first time we met, slacks and a short-sleeved shirt. His hair hadn't grown an inch. It was still combed up and over neatly and rather wetly from a surgical part into a mound that would have been out of fashion in any era. The part extended at a right angle across the back of his head. I had the feeling that if I looked closely enough I would be able to make out where the small tines of his comb had left off and the big ones had begun. When he stood up to gather his books he had a skinnier belt and a higher waist than I remembered. He was taller than Chip.

As they walked three abreast along Forbes Avenue, Ted also recalled that the other Chip was not especially talkative. The day the Livingstones had dropped Chip off at school, his new roommate had answered their questions thoughtfully, but he hadn't responded with any of his own questions or volunteered any information about himself. His idea of politeness seemed to be to regard even the most off-handed remark made by Teddy's parents as definitive. Still, he did exhibit one unimpeachable character trait on the present occasion: he was deeply and visibly impressed by his roommate's younger brother. For most of the way to the lab he walked with his head turned in Teddy's direction, following the early impressions of college life that Chip was soliciting from him. Since he was still absorbing his first day on campus, Teddy had to manufacture a few of the reactions he reported. But they were all generally well received. Likewise, during the lab, which began with a short lecture, Teddy was conscious of the other Chip's admiring gaze. In contrast to the history professor, this teacher announced Ted's presence in an accent of some kind and directed a few of his remarks to him. At the one point at which Teddy participated in the ensuing experiment, his brother's roommate could no longer contain himself. "I don't believe this," he said. "A high school junior sitting through a college biology lab?"

After the lab, out in the street, Chip's behavior took a strange although not unprecedented turn. It was only at that point, after he had taken me to my first college classes, that he seemed excited. However, I knew from long observation that when my brother got excited, he also became withdrawn. As the other Chip and I got involved in a conversation about a record we both owned, Chip walked alongside, silent and smiling, as though pleased with our performance. But his mind was obviously somewhere else.

Although it was only the second time that day and the third time in my life that I had entered Chip's dorm, the succession of stairs and fire doors we walked through on our way to the second floor already seemed the habit of a lifetime. We even kept a kind of formation, with someone different in the lead at every stage. When we reached the room Chip the Second walked over to his desk and reassumed his seat. Chip Livingstone crossed to the other side of the room. As his books bounced on the bed, I had two simultaneous insights. First, we had another stop to make. Second, Chip was sharing a room for the first time in his life. Or was that sharing a life for the first time in his room? In either case, he seemed to be taking the experience in stride.

"See you for dinner, Ches?" he asked with a jab of his forefinger at his seated roommate.

"Righto, Chas," he answered with a small salute.

"*You* may call me Chip," my brother said, rotating his finger in my direction. "Now, where did you leave the car?"

"On Ellsworth," I said.

"Ellsworth? Well, that was probably a good move," Chip said, "although now we have a walk ahead of us."

CHAPTER FOUR

Another Kind of Coach

"Funny," I thought as we walked along the sidewalk in shadow. "My shirt wasn't starched when I put it on this morning."

In the course of all the driving, walking and sitting I had done that day, my shirt had stuck to and come unstuck from my skin so often with sweat that it now felt stiff as a sail in the cool breeze of late afternoon. At the same time, inside my loafers my socks were beginning to feel somewhat mossy between my toes. I was following Chip in the other direction down Forbes Avenue, then up one of the innumerable side streets that led through the hospitals where huge slabs of stone were set down seemingly at random on the hillside. These few slanted city blocks resembled a quarry with street signs.

This seemed an unlikely route to a swimming pool, but I knew by now that was our destination. After we circled Pitt Stadium on a cobblestone street and climbed one last hill, we stood in front of Trees Hall. This structure was only a few years old and was regarded by area swimmers as the eighth wonder of the world. One of its wings housed a gym and the other an Olympic-size pool. I had been inside only once. (Six months earlier I had sat there in the stands to watch Chip win the 400 free at the regional high school championships when his archrival false started.) Today, however, we walked past the front steps where I had entered the building along with other knowledgeable Western Pennsylvania swimming fans.

Instead, we walked around the side of the building to a door by the loading dock where a janitor sat on the railing. Chip amused him with some remark that got sucked along with the corresponding laugh into a nearby and/or deafening fan. Inside, we followed a wide, humming gray hall past steel doors and cages. There was obviously a pool in the vicinity, because the cinder block of the walls smelled spongy with chlorine gas. After we climbed a set of echoing stairs we wound our way through an empty locker room and the dripping, subterranean-seeming showers, to come out on the pool deck.

From high in the stands the pool had looked like a distant

volcanic lake. At deck level it was different. I felt like an explorer on the shore of an uncharted lake. Chip and I hadn't spoken since we entered the building. The room we stood in was cavernous. At the far end of the pool, over the open water, the diving towers stood like indoor cliffs. I knew the pool was fifty-five by twenty-five yards—in other words, as wide as the pool at our high school was long. I learned later that a room to our right contained a pool the size of our high school pool that was used like a spare. In the empty, enormous space we padded across the tile deck toward the towers. In their shade, under the bleachers, were a couple of offices. The door we approached was completely covered with meet results, long lists of names and times. Under the taped-over window a plaque read, "COACH COHEN." Apparently, at the college level, even athletic staffs knew what alliteration was.

The office door opened (a little like a refrigerator door) into a soft, fluorescent glow. The room inside was white and antiseptic and (in fact) rather cool. A pleasant-looking man sat as though expecting us in a chair that swiveled towards the door. He looked more like a professor than Chip's history or biology teacher did. (The glasses and pipe helped.) True, there were no books to be seen on his desk or shelves, but papers and folders were stacked everywhere. A stop watch on a string lay on top of one pile like an old war medal. With a glance behind me, I noted that there were a couple of guys in tank suits and tee shirts already in the office. One was on a long table with his knees drawn up to his chest, and the other straddled a straight-backed chair. They nodded at Chip. At first I was afraid we had interrupted a conversation, but in the silence that followed my introduction I concluded there had been no conversation to interrupt.

From the seat Teddy chose for himself, that he assumed provisionally on the chilly tile floor, he soon realized he and Chip had not entered, much less created, an awkward silence. It was a voluptuous silence. Also, if this was not inconsistent, it was a sacred silence. No one felt the need to assert the reality in their midst: they were not at the moment working out. Rather, they made isolated allusions to practices past or to come, where they had swum poorly or could be expected to swim poorly. The conversation consisted entirely of punch lines. Coach Cohen would remove the pipe from his mouth long enough to issue a booming laugh in response to each reference, then reinsert it placidly. Teddy expected each of these guffaws to break the conversational logjam and introduce a more normal flow, but none did. Each time the office lapsed back into a meditative silence. Maybe it wasn't meant to be a discussion in the first place, just a testimonial to the coach, since he (after all) had devised these workouts. For his part, however, he acted as if he had no more control over a given practice than the swimmers did.

Another possibility was that this session was neither a conversation nor a tribute, but some bizarre kind of breathing exercise.

Whatever it was, Ted was apparently included. The feeling was only partially pleasant. On the one hand, as a novice he was under no pressure to contribute to the proceedings. On the other hand, he didn't quite see how he and/or his brother were going to get out of the office. The conversation did not seem to have ever begun; therefore, it could not end. From his corner by the open door he looked out over the becalmed pool, disturbed only by the eddy of the jets along its sides. The half dozen or so red-and-white lane markers that were set up for short course practice, i. e., across the pool, seemed to tremble slightly as though strung too tightly. The patterned surface of the water might have been reflecting trees instead of the ribbed concrete ceiling overhead.

Finally Chip asked, "Are the kids coming in tonight?"

"Yes, they are," Coach Cohen said, holding his pipe briefly at arm's length; and so far his every remark seemed facetious and ominous at the same time, if that was possible. "They should be here any time now. Are you getting in today?"

"I'll do a couple of thousand," Chip said.

Perhaps only Chip's brother could have detected the blush that accompanied that statement. With a certain complacency, snug in his tiled corner, he reflected that swimmers, who spent half their lives parading around in the skin-tight, transparent lingerie known as tank suits, were modest when you least expected it. However, Teddy immediately felt another emotion—namely, horror—as his brother turned in his direction. Along with everyone else in the room, Teddy recognized one of the moments that cropped up periodically out of the general insignificance of his life when he went from being a group's cipher to being its cynosure. "Do you want to swim with the team tonight, Teddy?" he was asked by his brother, who seemed in that instant a spokesman, a suppliant for his acquaintances in the office. Suddenly the success of this human encounter, the whole desultory dialogue Teddy had witnessed and had, truth to tell, been secretly deriding, depended on him.

Fortunately, with a barely perceptible pause, his brother burst out with, "You didn't bring a suit!" His observation touched off the gale of laughter that Ted had long sensed was being suppressed in the room. Nothing is so amusing to swimmers as narrowly averted exertion—even if it is not their own exertion that has been averted narrowly.

Besides redeeming the moment, the remark also freed Chip and me from the spell of the office. As we walked back along the deck toward the locker room, Chip explained that varsity swimming teams could not practice officially before a certain date. In a matter of a week or two Pitt's team would be working out in the early afternoon. In the meantime, he could continue to practice in the evening with the age-group team he had been swimming with for the past few years. Norm Cohen—everyone, I soon learned, even the youngest kids on the team, called him Norm—coached Pitt's team and ran the age-group program as well in Trees Pool over the winter and at an outdoor pool during the summer. These were the workouts that Chip had attended in preference those at Community Swim Club directed by his colleague, Ed Gow.

This time the locker room was full of screaming boys of all ages, including mine. I recognized a couple of my nemeses from the summer league meets. I probably looked as out of place to them as they did to me. To my mild disgust, my peers wrestled with each other as they undressed; they clanged the doors of their lockers shut like cymbals. Chip led me past this melee to the team locker room, a concrete alcove all the way to the back of the building, where he kept his suit. Still in my street clothes, I followed him like his manager back through the main locker room and showers and onto the pool deck. I kept walking past the deep end to a bench by the offices. Norm Cohen, now the only other fully clothed person in the place, strolled around the deck adjusting the pace clocks as one by one his swimmers threw themselves with one last mid-air writhe into the water.

With no more assignment than I had all day long, I got up

after a few minutes and found the stairs to the bleachers, directly behind me, over the offices. From the first row, ten feet or so above the deck, I surveyed the expanse before me. The team was using the closest half of the pool. The shallow end beyond, which in itself was larger than just about any body of water I had ever been in, remained a blank tranquil bay while the deep end seethed with swimmers, now well into their warm-ups. Gradually, everyone finished and coasted into the wall to hang onto the lane markers as Coach Cohen pulled a folding chair up to the edge of the pool and addressed them. By the time his words reached me they, as well as the occasional laugh, were nothing but garbled echoes; but he seemed to be giving each lane its own workout.

"On the top," he said as he stood up; that much I caught.

Chip and the two guys from the office (in a lane by themselves) set off on a set of one hundreds. They swam in a circle, up on one side of the lane and down on the other side, keeping to the right, four lengths at a time. As soon as they touched at the end of each hundred, they snapped their head up, all attention. For the few seconds before they pushed off again they were on their best behavior, watching the pace clock with the gravest respect. They left five seconds after one another and kept the same distance apart the whole way. At times they seemed synchronized, stroke for stroke. It wasn't as easy to distinguish Chip's freestyle here as it was at Community. Both his lane mates had the same smooth, high-elbowed form that he had.

Before long Teddy was mesmerized, his eyes stuck on the spectacle in front of him. The hum of the building that surrounded him might have emanated from the team, which Norm Cohen had set in motion like a machine. The dozen lanes of swimmers spun like so many chains in an elaborate transmission. Across the pool, sliding glass doors to a patio outside, wide open, disclosed the full strangeness of swimming indoors on such a day: sunlight lapped onto the tiles of the deck like gentle surf. No voice was any longer to be heard, although when the swimmers turned their heads to breathe you might have gotten the feeling they were interrupting an underwater conversation to do so.

On the other hand, maybe Teddy was the one underwater. He was feeling the backwash of the moment in the office when he was suddenly center stage. Only now did he fully recognize it as one of the clearings in his life that he stumbled into unaware and at wide intervals. For that second he was back in the woods, facing Progar, or hanging on the wall of Chapel Gate's locker room. Superimposed on the spinning pool, scenes from his past began to click through his mind like a slide show. A vision of a neighbor girl walking a collie dog down their street presented itself to him. The collar of her coat matched the collie's fur. He was watching her through the picture window of their house. The act of watching was part of the memory. Because that girl had been pretty, Cindy appeared to him next, although more as an idea than as an image, if there's any difference. He reflected that sometimes one memory recalls a similar one, but that other times the only thing two memories have in common is that you remember them both.

Yes, it was now official: his impression of the office and his present reflections belonged to the same moment. He was not straining the sensation. He was still simultaneously watching and remembering the scene in front of him. In fact, he was remembering it beforehand. He knew somehow that one day he would look back on many laps in this pool, swum separately, one stroke at a time, but recalled as a single act.

He wondered how many times before he had been in this mental state. . . five times, six times. . .not earlier that day, as he drove into Oakland, or sat through Chip's classes, or hiked up the hill; although now those acts reflected a little of his current condition, a glint of awareness-after-the-fact, which for all practical purposes is memory-in-advance. Maybe his vision of normality as he left his house that noontime had set off this whole train of thought. Teddy would concede the argument that Chip often advanced: no one's life was perfect, everyone's life was blighted. But at least there were these moments of asylum. How often would he feel this way again? Simple extrapolation suggested maybe fifteen more times. Life wasn't that long when you realized it consisted of twenty moments of consciousness.

It only made matters worse to consider that they were all the same moment.

The one thing I was not aware of in my heightened state of being was the presence with me in the bleachers of Norm Cohen. Apparently it was going to be a long set of hundreds, so the coach had time to walk around, pipe firmly in place. He sat on the same bench as I, but just far enough away that conversation on my part was clearly not obligatory and (in fact) might have been considered bravado. Coach Cohen had one of the more placid profiles that I had studied. Under thick black hair and glasses equally ebony, he had a slightly hooked nose, round cheeks and not the strongest of chins. Camel-like, he ruminated the scene before him. His physique was clearly that of a former swimmer, a breaststroker would have been my guess. There seemed no logical or anatomical connection between the broad shoulders and the pillow of gut over his belt as he slumped watchfully in his seat. I turned back to the pool and tried to empty my own gaze of everything but what he saw. I felt sure that neither girls nor collies in any combination had a place in the coach's mind's eye.

So it came as a surprise when he spoke.

"Do you think swimming is ninety percent mental?" he asked. "Or is that just an old coach's cliché?"

As I looked over to meet Norm Cohen's sidelong, open-mouthed stare, I wasn't sure whether he really required a hand to hold his pipe out there in front of his face, or whether it wouldn't just hang there in mid-air, cartoon-style. His question combined humor and threat in the same proportions as his other remarks had, so that, as before, my response was either critical or inconsequential.

"All clichés are true, aren't they?" I asked. "Or, what I mean is, they're all false, but they have to be true first before they can be false."

In answer, Coach Cohen exploded in laughter and swiveled back toward the pool. Teddy hadn't started out to say anything funny, but he was always happy to be credited with a witticism, especially by a coach. Since below them in the pool a number of lanes happened to be between hundreds at the same time, Coach Cohen took the pipe out of his mouth long enough to bellow, "Let's see some intensity, people!" The swimmers never took their eyes off the pace clock, as though it was an interpreter. Then, apparently as part of a new conversation, Coach Cohen asked, "Why didn't you go out for this team?"

"I don't know," Teddy said, because truthfully, he didn't know he was invited. "I guess we never took swimming as seriously

as Chip."

"Who's 'we?'" Norm Cohen asked, back on the brink of outrage.

"Billy and I. My other brother."

"Chip has two brothers?" the coach inquired with a grimace of enlightenment. "Bring him down with you."

CHAPTER FIVE

A Sort-of Post-Practice Double-Date

The walk back down the hill wasn't any easier than the walk up had been. Every time I dug my heel into the steep sidewalk I felt as though my next step would be into free fall. To no one's surprise (at least not mine) Chip had not just swum the couple of thousand yards he had announced, but he had done the team's whole workout. As we rounded Pitt Stadium, I told him what I had discussed with Coach Cohen while he was immersed.

"Norm Cohen suggested I try out for the team," I said.

"I thought of that," Chip said.

He didn't say when he had thought of it. His smile was distant and dreamy again.

“He said Billy should try out, too.”

“Billy? I’m not so sure about him.”

“Don’t forget, he was getting pretty good toward the end of the summer,” I said between the jolts of our descent.

“It’s not that he doesn’t have potential,” Chip said. “It’s a matter of timing. He’s a senior in high school this year, and who knows where he’ll be next year? I haven’t heard anything about him applying to Pitt. Any improvement he made under Norm would benefit his next coach. I’m in an awkward position. I would hate to make it seem like a favor to get Billy on the team. I’m mostly thinking of Norm.”

“It was his idea.”

As we pulled up on the level of Fifth Avenue, a thought struck Chip and he asked, “You’re staying for dinner, aren’t you?”

“I think so,” I said.

“Mom isn’t expecting you, I mean?”

“I don’t think so. I could call.”

“Don’t bother. She knows where you are.”

We crossed Fifth Avenue by the university book store and stood out front while Chip looked up and down the street. Students came out of the doors behind us carrying full shopping bags, as though they were coming from a grocery store.

“Now, we’re expecting two extra people for dinner.”

"Chip, right?" I asked. "Ches, that is."

"Right. And Susan."

"Susan?"

"A girl I met on the team. I guess she couldn't make practice tonight," Chip said. Then he looked at me and announced, "The University of Pittsburgh *is* a coeducational institution."

Fifteen minutes later we were sitting in a cafeteria in the basement of Chip's dorm. Across the table from me sat a pretty, small but solid girl named Susan Neeley. Earlier (outside the book store) we saw her walking along the sidewalk toward us in shorts and a windbreaker. When she greeted us, we turned and walked back with her in the direction from which she had come. It wasn't cool yet, although the evening was advancing. We walked head-on into sunlight as though into a breeze. Ches came straight downstairs from the room and joined us at our table. The cafeteria was reminiscent of the one at the high school, except that there were a lot of round tables instead of a few real long ones. I paid for my meal with coupons that Chip tore out of a book for me.

"So, Teddy, have you known Chip long?" Susan asked facetiously over her salad; and then she answered herself by saying, "I know, all your life!"

"It seems like longer," I said.

"It was longer," Chip said. "It was all my life."

“That doesn’t make any sense, honey,” Susan said, laying a hand on Chip’s knee and smiling sweetly.

With her jacket off she had more shape than I had at first suspected. Her shoulders were broad but her torso and hips compact; the boy’s tee shirt she wore was bunched in folds around her waist. Her shirt was white, but not as white as the bra underneath, like a shadow on snow. She was still tan. Her legs were smooth and muscular, with developed, detachable-looking calves. Her short brown hair, streaked with blonde, swirled when she turned her head like those pleated skirts of two different materials. She was from California, or at least her father was. I never got her family situation straight.

“I hope you approve of the company your brother is keeping in college,” she said to me.

“I’m just relieved you don’t call him ‘Chas,’” I said.

“‘Chas,’” she laughed, glancing at the other Chip, who was contentedly breaking saltines into a bowl of chili.

He seemed to have gotten all the talk out of his system earlier that day with me.

“No, that’s a roommate thing.”

I felt comfortable with Susan, and conversation never lagged, even though all four of us were seldom at the table at the same time. You could have all you wanted of certain items in the food line; and at some point, beginning almost immediately, everyone got up to get a refill of something or other. Susan was watching Chip make his way back from the milk station, an upright stainless steel cabinet with rubber spouts.

"You're allowed to fill your glass, Chip," she said. "It's an all-you-can-drink arrangement."

"All the more reason not to," he said, sitting down.

"Did you follow that?" Susan responded quickly and quizzically to me. "And we won't laugh at you if you spill some," she went on, although she was laughing at the moment.

Long since done with her meal, she had pushed her tray aside to rest her forearms on the table and observe Chip.

"Have you noticed that your brother never finishes a glass of milk, and he never fills one to the top?" she asked.

"Have you ever driven with him?"

Susan shook her head..

"That's right. He doesn't have a car here. Well, he also (on principle) will never fill the tank with gas. What's your maximum purchase, Chip? Five dollars?"

"That's plenty," Chip said.

Susan dropped her jaw, looking at me dumbfounded, in an attractive sort of way.

"It's not plenty if you're driving to Bismarck, North

Dakota," she said.

"Listen, if you're driving that far you're going to have to stop a lot of times for gas anyway. So what's the point of filling up?" Chip asked. "And why would you want to go to Bismarck, North Dakota?"

"It's the state capital," I explained.

"I think we could get you into this school with that kind of knowledge," Chip then retorted.

Susan had a funny way of looking at one person while she spoke to someone else. Just then she seemed to be laughing at the other Chip's reaction to our exchange rather than at the exchange itself. In turn, Ches was probably reacting for her benefit more visibly than he ordinarily would have. My brother was laughing too, but only from the cheekbones down. His eyebrows were contracted as though in an unrelated frown. Actually, this was the way I liked him best, amused but distracted, almost worried. The expression he had on his face usually meant that he was going to reveal something interesting about himself, something too strange but also too true to be embarrassing. You wouldn't think it logically possible that self-deprecation could be a person's most attractive quality. I was just pleased to know that Chip could act this way, not only in public, but also in the presence of a girl.

"Well, Chip," I said. "Does she know about it?"

"Know about what?" Susan asked.

"Consummation," I said.

"Consummation?" Susan inquired. "Sounds interesting."

"It's a theory Chip has," I explained.

"I thought I had heard all his theories," Susan replied. "But I haven't heard this one."

"You'd better explain it, Chip," I told Chip.

"Is this a theory just about milk and gasoline, or does it apply to all liquids?" Susan asked as she continued to her direct her questions to me.

"It's a wide-ranging theory," Chip said, cupping his hands around his glass and gazing into it, serious in spite of himself. "Naturally you don't want a glass of anything to be completely empty."

"How about if you're through with it?" Susan asked.

"But you don't want it to be completely full, either," Chip continued, "because, in a way, they're the same thing. If the glass can be full, it can also be empty. One extreme implies the other. I would even go so far as to say that if you fill a glass right to the top, you are inviting or even provoking it to be empty. It's best to maintain the level of the liquid in the middle someplace, between a third empty and a third full. You would certainly never wait until you had less than a full swallow left before you got some more."

"That all doesn't alter the fact that being full is a good thing, and being empty is a bad thing," Susan said.

(It had never occurred to me to test Chip's theories.)

"You just can't face the fact that something can be finished. But it can be," Susan added.

"On the other hand," Chip said, raising a finger, "what's so special about being full? That's just one point among many. It would be very difficult, and potentially messy, to find that exact point every time."

"It is special. It's an extreme. You just said so," Susan said. "You're contradicting yourself, sweetie."

"Well, then I must have been right the first time," Chip said.

The three of us looked at each other for a minute. Then Ches said, "I'm thirsty," and we all laughed.

"The mind of a distance swimmer," Susan sighed, brushing Chip's hair back from his forehead.

(He flinched when Mom did that.)

"Is that what you do to keep your mind off all those laps? Think up theories?" Susan asked.

"Actually, consummation does relate to swimming," Chip said. "It explains why I'd rather work out than race. Coaches always try to convince you that training is good. The harder and longer you practice, the better. But really (for them) it's just a means to an end. If it's such a good thing, why stop doing it?"

"I'll bet you're glad when a workout is over," Susan said.

"All that means is that I should be in better shape," Chip said.

"You're in great shape." Susan told Chip as she gave him a little shove with her hand, which she had dropped confidingly to his shoulder. "At least you look great in a tank suit, even that baggy one you insist on wearing. That's another thing about your brother, Teddy. Why does he wear such baggy tank suits?"

"More resistance," Chip said. "It makes me work harder in the water. It makes me feel slower than I actually am. Think how I'll feel when I take it off."

"Think how *I'll* feel when you take it off," Susan said, standing up. "Don't worry, Teddy. He wears another one underneath."

"I know."

"*And* I'm going to be late for my class," Susan said.

She kissed Chip not exactly on the cheek, but on the jaw next to his ear. Then she ruffled his hair, slid back her chair and stood up to leave.

"Class after dinner?" I asked.

"You're in college now, babe," Susan said as she ruffled my hair too, and waved to the table as she left.

We three guys talked for a little while longer, then got up and walked outside into twilight and started up the street. Ches had finished his homework for the day and was going to go read newspapers in the library. Chip ended up walking me all the way back to the car. We stood on the sidewalk on Ellsworth Avenue in front of big houses with deep front porches. (I decided growing up in one of them must give people a completely different outlook on life.)

"Do you want me to drive you back to your dorm?" I asked, feeling the car keys in my pocket.

"No, I'll walk," Chip said.

But he was in no hurry to get started. As I opened the door of the car and got in he stood rocking slightly on his heels, hands in his pockets. That meant no parting handshake, either, which actually was all right with me. Too final. Chip leaned against the car and spoke to me where I sat behind the steering wheel.

"You should really come down to practice," he said, "and bring Billy. Why not?"

CHAPTER SIX

A Day at the Office

On Tuesday, October 10, 1967, at approximately four o'clock in the afternoon, the unthinkable took place.

Teddy Livingstone was present at the time, but failed to grasp the significance of what he saw. He seemed to be making a career as unwitting eyewitness to history.

A week or so had passed since Teddy had visited Chip on campus. He had walked down the hill to the shopping center with Hooty after school, ostensibly to pick up a pair of re-heeled shoes for Mrs. Hurwitz. In actuality, the two adolescents walked the length of Fox Chapel Plaza, making a point to stop in every store but Nick's, the shoe repairman's. Then they crossed Fox Chapel Road and made a similar circuit around Fox Chapel Village, the home of Claber's and its satellite shops. In each of these places of business Teddy acted as their spokesman, due to his mastery of a single phrase, "Just browsing." This claim was more plausible in some establishments than in others—more so in the hobby store for instance than in the Swagger Shop, where a robust older woman with a torso under her knit dress like a made bed greeted them severely from behind a counter. (Of course, if he and Hooty had wanted to be taken seriously as customers of china, they wouldn't have dressed in army surplus.)

The two purchases they did make were related, a magazine from the rack of the Rexall drug store to be read over milkshakes at the Isaly's next door. Once (when the magazine was in Hooty's custody) Teddy glanced across the aisle to see his brother Billy sitting in another booth with his girlfriend, Debbie. The fact that Debbie was already looking Teddy fully in the eyes made any greeting on his part seem superfluous. Billy was looking down at the surface of the table (which unless Teddy was in error) supported no foodstuff beyond its shakers of salt, pepper and sugar. Teen-aged customers were not encouraged by the management of Isaly's to conduct either fasts or vigils on the premises; but this young couple would probably not be evicted so long as the store remained nearly empty, and their booth maintained its aura of sobriety.

A few minutes later, spontaneously, all four young adults got up and left the store together. On the sidewalk outside, however, they reconfigured in a kind of pantomime. Billy shrugged; and

Debbie, with a last, doleful look at Teddy, turned and walked away. Billy fell in step with Hooty and Teddy as they made way for Nick's to pick up Mrs. Hurwitz's refurbished shoes.

Billy and Debbie had broken up.

As Teddy recalled the event several days later, leaning meditatively on a rake, it was slightly blurred around the edges, as though he viewed it through the eye-holes of the mask of a fatuous former self. The idiotic smile with which he had bade Debbie farewell outside Isaly's seemed stuck on his mind's face like a cramp. Had he realized what was transpiring between Billy and his girlfriend, he would have interceded on someone's, on anyone's, behalf. He would have implored both parties to remember that they had been a couple since time immemorial, to consider how many of their acquaintances' world views would be shattered if they separated. He would further have asked Debbie with whom Billy was then supposed to spend all his time? Instead, he had acted as though it were any other weekday at the shopping center.

These afterthoughts were mildly ironic in light of what happened next.

Teddy was standing ankle-deep in fallen leaves in the back yard of one of his clients. These particular leaves—small, crisp and yellow—reminded him of corn flakes. They were his least favorite leaves to sweep up, because they constantly got stuck in the rake—

another quality they shared with corn flakes, if you substituted teeth for tines. They smelled not unlike corn flakes.

Teddy's professional gardening extended well into the autumn, but by then it amounted to little more than odd jobs—stacking wood, bringing in lawn furniture. He missed the routine of summertime when the grass had to be cut every week, every five days in some cases. Looking around, he concluded with something like regret that he might have mowed the Fikes' lawn for the last time that year. Leaves lay under their respective trees like so many throw rugs on a slightly threadbare green carpet. Under smooth, plaster-gray clouds, the Fikes' back yard had no more horizon than a living room. Over the next couple of weeks he would gather all the fallen and yet-to-fall leaves into an old bedspread—his father's method—and haul them into the woods. After the first cold rain the grass would be as slick as linoleum.

At this point in his survey of the yard Teddy saw Cindy.

She must have followed the stone walk that led around the side of the house. She stood at the very edge of the driveway, seemingly hesitant to walk into the yard, as though it was a lake that was very likely both deep and cold, unless the analogy would work better the other way around, with the asphalt parking area a pool out of which, like a nymph surprised in a state of undress, Cindy was loath to step.

What Teddy thought first as he looked at her was that she was as much a vision as a girl. Surprising as it was that she was there, it would somehow have been more surprising if she wasn't. She wore one sweater, a crew-neck, over another, a turtleneck. He wasn't sure he had ever seen her in blue jeans before this. Parted like a boy's hair, her light brown hair fell slant-wise across her forehead and hooked softly on one side under her chin. Her face was clearer, and more open than most skies, certainly more than presently overhead. As always, when he saw her Teddy was virtually certain that Cindy answered to his oldest idea of beauty—that he had formed instantly and retroactively the first time he saw her, the way a sound that wakes you up must sometimes improvise a dream to account for itself.

What he thought next was that this was his girlfriend.

What he said was, "What are you doing here?"

"I realized I had never seen you at work," Cindy said with a smile and/or shrug.

Teddy laughed and said, "A yard isn't like an office, you know. You can enter without knocking."

"Your mother told me how to find the house."

Still, Cindy stayed where she was. She was jingling something in her hands. It was car keys. (She had turned sixteen earlier in the month.) Behind her the open garage glittered with the tools of Teddy's trade. The Fikes were retired. Their children had long since vanished into adulthood, and they never seemed to work in the yard. Nevertheless, every conceivable lawn implement had its place on the pegboard walls inside the garage. Although, or since, the house was utterly still, Teddy would naturally have assumed that Mrs. Fike was upstairs training binoculars on him, had she not at just that moment emerged from the porch door and struck out across the yard toward him.

"You have a friend," she said in mid-stride; and her tone was not so much hostile as incredulous, which when you thought about it was probably worse.

Teddy watched what ensued in wonder. Mrs. Fike led Cindy around the yard, pointing out its various amenities, while Teddy followed in a semi-proprietary way. Without necessarily implying any great knowledge of gardening on her part, Cindy asked all the right questions and made all the right comments. In the course of this tour, Mrs. Fike delivered, albeit to Cindy, her first recorded compliment on Teddy's work. He left no corners at all when he edged a flower bed. She came down hard on that 't' in "at all"—or is that "a tall?"—as she did in "often.")

Finally, having ended up in the back yard again, Mrs. Fike said to Teddy, "Why don't you take your friend for a walk? We have such a nice trail behind the house, don't you know?"

Although Teddy did know, he thanked her anyway. But then in his guise of polite employee, he would have thanked her for instructions to hose down the driveway.

The Fikes' house was the biggest in the development, a two-story frame among brick ranches. At the end of its street, its back yard was notched into the woods. The path that Mrs. Fike had alluded to was a shortcut to any number of destinations. No one knew for sure whether the Fikes objected to its light but steady traffic. As a precaution, neighborhood kids followed the boundary between their property and the Politos' next door so as to be legally in no one's yard if accosted before they reached the cover of the trees.

Teddy set his rake against a tree and motioned Cindy toward the woods as the porch door clattered shut behind Mrs. Fike. Single-file, they followed the trail, which was flat at first and edged with split rails dug and now decomposing into the ground. Under the light gray sky, the trees were bright and feathery with their last leaves. To the best of Teddy's knowledge, the woods had never been raked.

"What are you thinking?" Cindy asked.

"Can I tell you later? It wasn't too interesting."

"But then you won't be thinking it," Cindy said. "You'll be remembering it."

"I mean, when I'm thinking something else."

For answer, a handful of leaves bounced off Teddy's back.

"You've never played in these woods, have you?" Teddy asked after a minute.

"I've never played in woods," Cindy said. "Where I grew up we had parks. Do you even have parks here?"

"I can think of a baseball field," Teddy said. "Does that count?"

They were in what he thought of as the stump room of the woods. From one of the several stumps in the clearing you could at one time have launched yourself outward on a thick, hoary vine—until the day it collapsed under the weight of one Hooty Hurwitz, who had arced impassive as a meteor through the air to the ground below him. Teddy saw this happen.

"We played here all the time, although I never exactly recognize anything. I don't know if it's because I'm always in a slightly different place, or because it's a different time, or if there's any difference." Teddy said as he stopped and turned around. "There. I just thought that. Aren't you glad you asked?"

"I didn't," Cindy said.

One reason Teddy had stopped was that they were on top of the cliffs. Although they wouldn't have seemed as towering to you as they had when you were six years old, you still would not have wanted to do a swan dive off them into the creek below, a foot and a half deep at flood tide. As Teddy led the way down a steep path off to one side, Cindy grabbed a sleeve of his sweatshirt and gave a short, charming shriek.

At the bottom she asked, "What kind of games did you play when you were children? 'I know—let's play Death March today.' Can't we sit down?"

They found two flat rocks at the base of the cliffs, one slightly higher than the other. They sat cross-legged, not quite facing each other, as though on two ice floes that might crack and drift apart at any moment. A rustling silence settled around them. The creek behind them led upstream to Billy's swimming hole, closed like Community Swimming Club for the winter, unless Billy had devised some heating system for it, and/or had it domed, which was not totally beyond the realm of possibility.

"Someone proposed to me here once," Teddy said. "You know her. Cathy Dahlem."

"Not your type," Cindy said.

"We were nine and eight, respectively. I turned her down immediately. I was nice about it."

"I'm so glad," Cindy said.

"For what?" Teddy asked, "that I declined, or that I was nice about it?"

"I knew you'd be nice," Cindy said.

Teddy was thinking that it was pleasant just to sit.

"Why don't girls have summer jobs?" Cindy asked.

"Girls work at the pool," Teddy said.

"But they don't do anything. They sit at the front desk. They pour Coke at the snack bar."

"They get paid; therefore, they work," Teddy said. "Anyway, what do lifeguards do? They sit."

"They have responsibility," Cindy said.

Enough branches were bare that you could make out the surrounding terrain. Hills sloped away from the creek on both sides. The leaf-strewn ground showed tawny and speckled through the trunks of the trees like a hide. Directly behind them the cliffs crouched sphinx-like.

"It's nice to have a job," Cindy said. "It's better than just getting an allowance."

"That's what my father says," Teddy said. "Or rather, I think that's what he would say if you asked him."

"Not mine," Cindy said.

After another minute, Teddy got up and dusted off his pants. "You gave me an idea," he said. "Let's go."

"I was just getting comfortable," Cindy pouted.

"No, you were just getting numb," Teddy said. "These rocks

are hard."

With Teddy in the lead again they began to follow the creek, crossing it at a couple of points to keep to the flatter bank. Soon they struck back into the woods along a faint path. Teddy discouraged Cindy from testing any of the vines they passed on the ground because even she outweighed the ten-year-old Hooty Hurwitz. But this was palpable rationalization. They weren't sight-seeing anymore. They had a destination.

Eventually, Cindy plucked at the back of Teddy's sweatshirt and said, "Remember, I'm not in shape. I don't do sports during the school year."

"It's not much farther," Teddy said.

"What exactly do you have in mind?" Cindy asked.

"I'm planning a traditional activity," Teddy told her, "one with a twist."

"Tell me now."

Cindy's voice was suddenly distant, literally. Teddy turned around to see that she had stopped in the middle of the path.

"All right. If you don't want to be surprised," he said. "Skinny-dipping."

Cindy stood stock-still, like a started deer. Her nostrils all but flared. "I'm lost," she said. "I've been lost since we left the yard. I couldn't find my way back if I turned around right here."

"Skinny-dipping is a very traditional activity," Teddy said as he employed his most transparently plausible tone, the one he reserved for teachers and his mother; and it always worked: Teddy alone among his contemporaries seemed to have discovered that you could confess an adult into submission. "Besides, we're going to do it in reverse."

"That's not funny, Teddy, or fair, even if it was hot outside."

"You'll understand," Teddy said.

Cindy approached him warily, stopping short of his outstretched hand.

"Come on. We're almost there."

Fifty yards farther along the path they broke into a clearing and came up against the corner of a cyclone fence. On the other side, a stone grill stood at the center of a grove of shade trees.

"Where are we?" Cindy asked.

"You know where we are," Teddy told her. "Look around."

They had emerged from the woods at the rear of Community Swim Club, the time-honored skinny-dipper's approach. At this point the fence was built into a small slope that gave a leg up to the trespasser. Furthermore, this section of fence was reinforced with a crossbar, a natural foothold for the descent. Along the top bar, several strands of wire were permanently bent back.

"The pool's empty, Teddy," Cindy said with a smirk, as much out of relief as of sarcasm or complicity. "We can't skinny-dip."

"That's the twist," Teddy said. "Clothes, no water."

Wedging the toe of his tennis shoe into the wire mesh, Teddy clambered over the fence, then helped Cindy, who from that point on was game. They strolled over all the decks, which were bare and bone-dry around the empty concrete socket of the swimming pool. The snack bar, boarded up for the winter, could have been the loading dock of a warehouse. Laughing, Teddy and Cindy lay down side by side on a grassy slope, sunbathing in street clothes. If you lay still and strained you could feel a flush on your forehead under the cool breeze.

"Come on," Teddy said, sitting up. "If we don't actually get in the pool this won't count as skinny-dipping, not even as reverse skinny-dipping."

He walked down to the pool deck and hopped into the shallow end. Over-cautiously perhaps, Cindy climbed down the three steps of the nearest ladder.

"Now, pick a lane," Teddy said. When they each stood at the end of the pool on one of the lines painted on the bottom, Teddy began the familiar tripartite command with a "judges and timers ready." At the "go," he and Cindy started off at a stroll down the

length of the pool.

"You can swim faster when you leave out the water," Cindy said. "Did you bring a stop watch?"

"Look," Teddy said, turning around and walking backwards.

"What are you doing?" Cindy said.

"Backstroke, of course."

"Meanwhile, I won," Cindy said, laying a hand on the far wall.

Next, they walked over to the brink of the deep end, which was partly full of rain water, brown and brackish with sodden leaves. Since they were already five feet down into the pool, the water was only a few feet below them. Still, it was a little like being on the edge of the cliffs again.

"From where did that water come?" Cindy asked.

"Some leaves clogged the drain, probably," Teddy said.

"It's scary. You can't tell: the water might go down forever. If you fell in you might not be able to get out. You couldn't reach the ladders."

"You could climb up this side. It might be slippery, but you could make it," Teddy said as he extended one foot to test the surface of the bottom as it slanted down to the drain.

"Don't," Cindy implored, wrapping both her arms around one of his.

They turned and walked back into the sunken stage of the shallow end. It echoed with absence—of water, of the crowd that had filled the club a few months before for the championships, a crowd of which Teddy had been a constituent part.

Teddy stopped and nearly faced Cindy and asked, "Did you have anything to say to me today?"

"You mean, like propose?" Cindy asked.

"The way you just appeared like that," Teddy said, "I thought maybe you had something important to say to me."

"No, nothing special."

"I just wondered."

They climbed out of the other end of the pool. On their way back to the fence they passed the filter room, and they looked at each other again.

"Your brother is strange, Teddy," Cindy said. "I know you admire him."

"Which one?"

"I'm talking about Chip."

"I know. 'Which one' is my standard response to any statement about either of my brothers," Teddy said. "To be honest, it did look funny when you two came out of the filter room together that time."

"It was even funnier than it looked," Cindy said. "Chip had

never so much as looked at me all summer. Then he takes me aside for a private pep talk."

"It worked. You swam well."

"For me."

"Do you remember the last relay?" Teddy asked.

"Of course I do," Cindy said. "We won."

"We lost."

The image of Billy stepping down off the block in favor of Chip unspooled again for Teddy like a film clip without its soundtrack. Come to think of it, that's the way he had experienced it in the first place.

"That's right, we really lost," Cindy said. "Chapel Gate was disqualified. We won the meet."

"Yes, we won," Teddy said.

The trip back to Fikes' didn't take as long, since they bypassed the cliffs. Dusk was settling on the trees. They walked quickly and quietly, Teddy pulling back branches and handing them to Cindy. The best of all possible situations awaited them at the Fikes' house. The Fikes car was gone from the garage, so they arrived unobserved. Teddy walked Cindy across the back yard. As before, she stood on the driveway while Teddy stayed behind in the cool and/or damp grass. Cindy cupped her car keys in her hands.

"Thank you for letting me visit you at work," she said.

"You're welcome."

"I won't do it again."

CHAPTER SEVEN

A Philosophy of Waking Up

It occurred to Teddy when he woke up one day the following week that the conditions were ideal for suicide.

Lately, more often than ever, before he woke up spontaneously, he opened his eyes in the grayness of early morning as though he had just blinked instead of slept for eight hours. Naturally, he had always found renewed consciousness less repugnant than Billy did. Even at this moment his brother, lying on his back with his head wrenched sideways on the pillow, seemed to be staring appalled straight through eyelids that were strained shut against the specter of the day to come. It would take every alternate effort on the part of Teddy and his mother to get him up for breakfast. In the past, Teddy had usually been awakened by some sound or smell, even if it was just the warm rusty breath of the furnace coming on in the morning. Sometimes the first thing he heard was Chip in the bathroom next door getting ready for his pre-school swimming practice. That seemed to be the only musical moment of Chip's day.

This morning he had simply and all at once been aware. Steely sunlight pried at the edges of their curtains, even a glance in that direction turned the interior of the room into a negative of itself. The dressers, the pants hung over the backs of chairs shone silver on black until your eyes readjusted. In the growing daylight, the dial of their electric clock could still just barely be termed luminous. Outside, the neighborhood fell open like a book. You could tell that it would be clear and cold, that frost would curl the grass in lawns up and down the street. The lid of a milk box, on their doorstep or a neighbor's, thudded shut. After precisely the proper interval, the motor of the milkman's truck revved.

Teddy could think of no sense impressions he would rather have as his last.

Conversely, and less selfishly, it would be a service to creation to fix it for all eternity at its most typical.

In addition, if he killed himself on a Tuesday, he would not be squandering a weekend.

Best of all, his suicide would appear utterly unmotivated. Sanguine by nature, he was currently enjoying perhaps the most profitable period of his life. He did well in school, and his social life was full. Unexpectedness was the hallmark of Teddy's recurrent fantasy of self-immolation. His friends and relatives must all be left shaking their heads. Perplexity should all but outweigh grief.

They had discussed the concept of gratuitous murder in his English class in connection with Crime and Punishment. Teddy liked their teacher, a consumptive-seeming recent college graduate named Mr. Hudak, who was given to sudden pauses in his lectures and quite possibly in his circulation. Unlike most of Teddy's teachers, he seemed to read in his spare time. Sitting on his desk one day with a knee drawn up to his chest, gazing cadaverously out the window, Mr. Hudak launched into an encyclopedic yet apparently impromptu discussion of suicide. Although he had taken no notes—he was too interested—Teddy could reconstruct the lecture point-for-point. Mr. Hudak had begun by citing the view of a French writer named Albert Camus that people face only one philosophical question in life, whether or not to kill themselves; i. e., one's decision to live commits one to a whole series of subsequent and secondary decisions. Shortly before he drank the prescribed hemlock, Socrates argued against suicide on the ground that human beings are on duty as God's sentries and that killing oneself would be tantamount to going AWOL. Soren Kierkegaard gave this military analogy a twist. The Danish philosopher maintained that people come into the world with sealed orders; i. e., human beings have a mission, but only God knows what it is. To judge from this survey, one citizen from every country had at some point stepped forward with a position on the subject of suicide. However, Teddy could remember in Mr. Hudak's roster neither an American nor any mention of gratuitous suicide. His conceiving and then executing the concept ought to be worth some extra credit.

In cold truth, the most pressing question Teddy confronted at the moment was whether or not he had the energy to get up and go to the bathroom.

CHAPTER EIGHT

The Definition of a Best Friend

When I said that my relationship with my brother Billy was no paragon of normality, what I probably meant was that it was only when it seemed normal that I worried about it. We could go for days on end without seeing each other at school. The senior homerooms were on a different floor, and our class schedules never brought either of us into the other's vicinity. Since I seemed to have an aversion to arriving anyplace at the last minute, I ordinarily walked down the hill to the bus stop with Hooty or some other friend instead of waiting for Billy. One leg stretched out on the long back seat of the bus, I would watch in comfort through the grilled window of the emergency exit as Billy rounded the curve of the road and sprinted the home stretch. Also, despite the several climate changes of a typical morning (as we ferried ourselves from home to bus to school) I tried never to break into a sweat before gym class.

On this particular morning I was standing with some friends

in the hall by the door of my homeroom before the first bell of the day. Obviously (as a group) we had answered life's sole philosophical question in the affirmative, and with the minimum existential anguish. The conversation turned to dating, or rather had not turned from it since yesterday. Now that I had a girlfriend I was consulted on the subject more often than I formerly was. Cindy was a few homerooms down the hall. She and I confined our dealings in the morning to a seemly wave. On schedule, Bill Leffler was rolling up the sleeves of his shirt. (I preferred to wait to do that until fourth period, when the day was safely over the hump and I had some feeling back in my fingers.) At present, the palms of my hands throbbed against my thighs through the material of my pants pockets. This year I was going to *have* to get a pair of gloves. I decided it was better to have hands that felt furry and smelled like socks for a period or two than to contract frostbite every morning.

At some point my milling classmates began to be sucked back into their homerooms like water molecules into the fibers of paper towels animated in certain TV commercials. Just then Billy walked by and spoke to me. Before I had time to react, we exchanged a few sentences. The gist was that the three of us—he, Hooty and I—would start going down to Oakland to swimming practice that evening after school. The bell, situated on the wall conveniently close to my cochlea, ratified this resolve with an earsplitting ring. Simultaneously, Mr. Emrick began his ritual closing of the homeroom door. He liked to grip it by the hinges with his fingertips and squeeze, so that it started to swing slowly inward, picking up speed as it went. This practice, along with his liberal use of the pointer during his history classes, probably accounted for his exceptional forearm development. He was a new teacher, although not a particularly young one. He might easily have concluded from this scene that Billy and I were friends rather than brothers.

Beginning that night, we drove down to Oakland three times a week—on Tuesday, Thursday and Saturday—to train with the AAU team under Coach Norm Rose. Usually Pitt's team would just be getting out of the pool as we arrived, so that we saw Chip in passing. We picked him out of the dripping, chiseled torsos that we threaded our way through on our way to the pool as though through a sculpture garden after a rain, with tank suits in place of fig leaves. But sometimes the collegians ran late, and our workouts overlapped.

Any resemblance between these sessions and those I was used to at Community Swim Club or the high school was purely coincidental. From the minute the three of us parked our car behind Trees Hall and walked around the pool side of the building, where chlorinated steam blasted through brick with the force of a thousand laundry rooms, we entered the wet, gray world of the age-group swimmer. Once we had our suits on, we gravitated in groups of four or five to one of many lanes where we spent the next couple of hours swimming around and around in circles. All you ever saw was a splash of feet ahead of you and an occasional tank suit blurring by on either side. All you heard was the pulse of a hundred flutter kicks and the echo of your own exhaling. Your ears, like two private grottos on the side of your head, each seemed to contain its own trickling stream. Every so often you could stop at the end of your lane and look at the clock for a few seconds before you set off again. In that respect, practice was a lot like school, only more humid.

Not all three of the age-groupers could make it to every practice. Various conflicts with school activities arose. Colds were caught. Billy's attendance was probably the best of the trio. He didn't have Debbie to see daily anymore, and he hadn't replaced her within the week, as everyone expected him to do. One Thursday Teddy and Hooty went down to practice alone. The November day was dark but warm, obviously on one end of winter, although it could just as easily have been a day in March. The threat of rain overhead seemed hollow. Against the high gray background, the wispy low black clouds looked more like smoke than coming rain. The practice was lightly attended, so afterwards Hooty and Teddy had a shower room and an entire aisle of lockers to themselves.

"You know what scientific discovery I just made today?"

Teddy asked.

"What?" Hooty retorted.

"I discovered where the fewest nerve endings per square inch on your body are."

"Where?"

"Here. On your lats."

Seated on a bench, Hooty interrupted his toweling off of his feet so as to give Teddy his undivided attention.

"You know how every time you put on your shirt—you think you're dry, you know—and your shirt sticks to your back right there?" By way of demonstration, Teddy squirmed. "You miss that spot when you dry off because it doesn't feel wet, ergo, no nerve endings. I'm telling Mr. Veltri. I'm giving a report in biology class."

"Schedule an assembly," Hooty said; and although he had just dried them off, he brushed the soles of his feet with his hands before he put on his shoes and his socks.

"Press conference," Teddy said.

As Hooty stood up and the two friends marched in strides out of the locker room, he said, "I don't care if I stink as a swimmer. I like the showers down here. Nice spray."

Hooty made this confession cheerfully, more like a resolution. His good humor proved infectious. By the time he and

Teddy reached the lobby and their lungs inflated with the first chemically untreated air of the last couple hours, their stride become a swagger. Teddy did not presume to contradict Hooty's claim that he stank. As a rule he did not discourage self-deprecation in his friends. (He also realized the hidden meaning of Hooty's remark was that he didn't mind if Teddy swam faster than he did.)

When they stepped out under the overhang of the front steps of the building, Hooty turned his head sharply and said almost to himself, as though recalling some catch phrase or quoting a favorite cartoon character, "Are it raining?"

(In fact, a few drops of rain had splattered on the sidewalk ahead of them with roughly the frequency and volume of popcorn in its early stages.)

Hunching his shoulders inside his jacket, Hooty said, "Kee-moan."

That quotation Teddy did recognize. He and Hooty were as far as they knew the only two listeners willing to acknowledge publicly that what the Beatles actually said in one of their most popular songs was not, "Come on, come on," but "Kee-moan, kee-moan."

As he jogged along beside Hooty to their car, Teddy was filled with the conviction that no human being had ever had a better ten minutes than his best friend Hooty had just logged; and that he was to some degree not simply a party to, but responsible for them. And the most admirable of all Hooty's gestures was that he never alluded to, nor let alone apologized for their falling out over the summer.

CHAPTER NINE

Two Philosophies of Working Out

Another day I went down to swimming practice by myself. Hooty was playing in a piano recital that night, and Billy's math club was holding its monthly meeting after school. Unlike my teammates, I was not cursed with well-roundedness. With nothing better, or else to do, I drove down to Trees Hall early, arriving long before the other age-groupers, while the university squad was still in the middle of their workout. My vantage point at poolside was much the same as it had been the day I visited Chip on campus, but this time the atmosphere was all business.

The whole team was on hand. Since swimmers occupied the deep end, the divers were off in one corner of the deck, vaulting from a portable one-meter springboard into a pile of foam rubber. Wearing a waist harness, one diver after another left the board with a deafening twang. A coach ran alongside, yelling commands and yanking on the rope attached by pulleys overhead to the harness. I watched Chip's friend Susan do a one and a half with several twists; I lost count. She wore a tee shirt and gym shorts. She was still tan. As she sprang, a tendon that ran the length of her leg stood out like the stripe on a pair of formal trousers.

Pipe in hand and/or mouth, Norm Cohen walked out of his office at random intervals to check on the workout in progress in the pool. Like all his swimmers, I had already developed a keen scent from the water for his blend of tobacco. As often, almost every lane was doing something different. The distance swimmers, of whom Chip was one, swam more or less continuously. Next to them, the stroke men bobbed and jerked through breast stroke and butterfly. The sprinters, nearest me, had the most leisure. They swam hard, but they took a lot of rest between sets.

I noticed one guy in this group in particular. Twice in the space of ten minutes, without seeming to ascertain the whereabouts of Coach Cohen either by sight or by smell, he bellowed from the pool, "Hey, Norm. I'm tight. I'm taking a shower." He would spring with a huge splash out of the pool, as though crashing through a pane of water, and stroll along the deck toward the locker room. Although he had left the sprinters' lane, he might when he came back drop in with the strokers and do a few lengths of fly until it was time for his next shower.

Eventually the distance swimmers paused for more than ten seconds. At the end of a long, steady set, their circle splintered into human flotsam. Swimmers drifted at random in the lane, paddled on their backs. Most of them finally dragged themselves out of the pool and staggered toward the locker room or the water fountain on the wall. One guy lay down on his back on a bench with one arm draped across his eyes and the other trailing on the deck. Chip spotted me from the water and waved limply. Hauling himself up the nearest ladder, he walked over and sat down beside me.

"Two-hundreds are the worst," he said. "They're not a sprint, they're not distance. They just hurt." Then he leaned into me damply and conspiratorially and nodded toward the locker room. "Look. There's Progar."

I turned my head in surprise. I had no idea that Progar went to Pitt. I had yet to recognize him among the varsity swimmers. I still didn't recognize him. The only person I saw in the direction Chip indicated was the sprinter I had observed earlier, once more on his way back from the showers. He was not only a compulsive bather, he was a compulsive loosener-up. With every step he twitched a limb away from his body. Muscles writhed on his arms and thighs like eels. He had a certain type of swimmer's physique, a wide upper body so flat it was slightly concave set like the blade of a shovel on the handle of his hips. When you saw him from the front in his proverbial band-aid of a bathing suit you had to assume that when he turned around a generous cross-section of his buttocks would be exposed; but in fact, from the back there was only the hint of a crack, which might have been no more obscene than the hollow of a nether vertebra. It was as though he had a split-level waist, higher on one side of his body than on the other. Either that, or he had tucked his cheeks into his suit like the tails of a shirt.

"Do you believe in the transmigration of souls?" Chip went on and asked.

"Depends what it is," I said.

"It's the theory that after death your soul survives to inhabit a different body, a better or worse one according to the kind of life you led."

"Oh," I said. "I haven't given it much thought. It doesn't sound very Presbyterian."

"Well, Plato believed in it," Chip said. "We just learned that in western civ. No wonder he has such a good reputation. He was right. If anything, he understated the case. He didn't realize that souls transmigrate while their owners are still alive. Although I haven't been keeping up with the obituaries."

The glance I directed at my older brother, while respectful, must have contained some skepticism.

"You have to look real close," he said. "He has a new body, even a new name—Leo Fichter. But he's still Progar."

"Then how did you recognize him?" I said.

Chip closed his eyes and leaned back against the wall. Expression drained from his face, and he seemed to attain a mystic's detachment from his surroundings. I personally would have preferred a bed of nails to clammy tile.

"I suppose I knew all along I would never escape him, that he would be here waiting for me. There's always a Progar. In every pool, on every team, there's always a guy I have to beat."

"But that's good, isn't it?" I asked. "It's good to have a challenge. You have to swim faster. And you beat Progar."

He had, and he hadn't.

"I don't go with that challenge stuff," Chip said. "It's self-defeating. Wouldn't the object be to always find an insuperable opponent? If you win a race, that means you failed to find a big enough challenge. You should always lose. You're not supposed to win."

"Well, then doesn't that fit right in with your theory of consummation? What better way to postpone perfection?"

"I admit it has some appeal in that light," Chip said, ready as ever unexpectedly to concede a point against him. "But I don't see why things can't just turn out the way you want. I'll revise my theory: Beyond Consummation." He paused. "It's just, why is there always somebody exactly the same speed as you?"

"I've wondered about that," I said. "Maybe because right from the start people compare themselves to other swimmers. They expect to just barely beat some record, that's all they want, so that's all they do, or they barely miss it; and then the same swimmers become coaches and pass on their expectations."

"I don't mean historically or psychologically," Chip said. "I mean why is life the way it is? Either things are the way you want them or they're not. It might as well be one way as the other."

"But there are so many ways things can go wrong," I said. "Whereas there's only one way they can go right. It's not exactly a fifty-fifty proposition."

"I guess what I'm trying to say is that you like to think you're unique. The whole time you're swimming you think, 'No one is working out as hard as I am; therefore, no one can be as fast as I am.' Only to find out that somebody else in a different pool has been working out just as hard as you and with exactly the same goals. So you're not unique, you're just like this other guy. Or rather, swimming is the only thing you have in common with him. You were doing that right, but everything else about you is wrong. You live in the wrong place. You read the wrong books. You should have a different favorite color. Your grandfather should have been a

Romanian freedom fighter."

"A Romanian freedom fighter?" I asked.

"It turns out that you *are* unique. You're uniquely wrong." Then Chip opened his eyes and asked, "Am I contradicting myself again?"

"It's hard to tell," I said.

"That probably means I am." He closed his eyes again and said, "I want to be a college swimmer."

"You are a college swimmer," I said.

"I mean, I want to swim in the meets, not just make the team. I want to letter as a freshman. In order to do that, I'll have to swim the two hundred. It's odd. We have a couple of good distance men and a couple of good sprinters, but we have no two hundred specialist. That's where there's an opening for a freestyler. The problem is, Fichter can swim it, too. He and I come at it from different directions. He's basically a sprinter, so for him the two hundred is a distance event. I'm a distance swimmer, so for me it's a sprint. It's an interesting event, I have to admit. It's neither here nor there. Schollander says you can pace it. He pushes the third fifty." He paused resignedly, dreamily adding, "Fichter is versatile."

A towel draped across her neck boxer-style, Susan walked by our bench and tapped Chip on the patella. If she was checking his reflexes, she should have been reassured when he sat up with a jerk.

"Get your rear in gear, son," she said without breaking stride. "The divers are done for the day."

"See you for dinner?" Chip asked.

"Class," Susan said.

"After class?" Chip called after her, a hand raised like an eager student. "After after class?"

With her hand on her chin and her eyebrows arched in a parody of deliberation, Susan disappeared into the girls' locker room. On cue, Norm Cohen emerged from his office, taken aback at something.

"We're not done yet, gentlemen," he said darkly.

Chip got up and dropped into the pool. He lay lifeless on the bottom for a minute, then surfaced and took his place in his lane.

A few minutes later, Leo Fichter, currently a backstroker, apparently felt the need for further ablutions. Eschewing the nearest ladder, he muscled himself up out of the pool and sauntered along its edge toward the showers while at his feet his teammates turned the water to froth with their flutter kicks. His receding back had the shape and rippling motion of a manta ray.

As in the past, Teddy must have become mesmerized by the circling swimmers, because when next he looked around Fichter was sitting beside him on the bench.

"I don't like to kick," he said.

Not only Leo's proximity, but also the fact that they were the only two people visible on dry land, argued that he was speaking to Teddy. However, he was gazing straight ahead of him into the middle distance while he somewhat irritably twisted from the waist and grabbed at his back, as though once he got the proper grip he would be able to unscrew his upper body. For lack of a response to Fichter's stated aversion—neither commiseration nor agreement seemed completely appropriate—Ted turned back to the pool, where the swimmers, their heads out of the water, gripped their kickboards like lecterns. But they couldn't think of anything to say, either.

"See, I'm a sprinter," Leo went on. "I have natural speed. Some people can only go so fast, no matter how hard they train. I can only go so slow. I can't go slower than a fifty-four in the hundred free no matter how bad of shape I'm in; and if I work out too hard, I only get tired."

Teddy realized then, although he had never before seen Leo Fichter, he had heard his name, whispered over the years through the ranks of swimmers at meets like a rumor of war. He had been a phenom, a child prodigy. From a suburb on the far side of the city, he had swum for Norm Cohen seemingly from the cradle. He still held some national record for eleven and twelve year-old boys, the hundred butterfly, as Teddy recalled. He had posted a time with which most college swimmers would be pleased. Ted was not sure Fichter himself had bettered it since. It was uncanny to see a 53.4, or whatever the record was, become flesh. Up close Teddy could make out Fichter's faint sideburns composed of silky hairs longer than those on his head, which were cropped into a swimmer's crew cut. He spoke with a slight lisp.

"What about the two hundred free?" Teddy asked. "You wouldn't exactly call that a sprint."

You wouldn't if your brother had just told you it wasn't one. With his observation Ted was both exercising the opinion he had just acquired from Chip and attempting to certify that a conversation and not a soliloquy was in progress. He was confident that Fichter would not detect his double motive. Then too, Teddy could not deny that he was flattered to be the recipient of a legend's philosophy of life, especially when it came on the heels of his brother's.

"Don't you need stamina as well as speed for that event?" Ted persisted in asking.

"Either you swim the two hundred or you don't," Leo said, not that informatively.

Still the only eye contact between them had been of the peripheral variety. Suddenly, shifting his weight, Fichter turned away from Teddy and grabbed at the other side of his waist, as though to test whether his torso might not turn counterclockwise rather than clockwise after all.

"You're little Livingstone, aren't you?" he asked after a minute.

"Yes," Teddy conceded.

"You're brother's great in workouts. You know that?"

While he uttered this seeming compliment, Fichter nodded toward the pool in obvious disapproval. The swimmers had skipped their kickboards clattering along the pool deck like stones on a tile pond, then wedged styrofoam pull-buoys between their thighs and pushed off for a stroke drill. In the course of most practices Chip worked his way up through a circle, and now he led his lane. He charged into the wall at the end of each hundred, while his teammates were content to glide into the finish and stack up behind him, hanging on the rope, until they set off again.

"I think he enjoys practice," Teddy said.

"That's what I said," Leo responded, although Teddy doubted a transcript of their conversation would back up Fichter. "He leaves his races in practice. See, he's the exact opposite of me. He's a workout swimmer. I'm a meet swimmer. I swim my best when it means something."

As he sat by Fichter and watched Chip tunnel ever farther into his workout, Teddy recalled the question Susan had asked his brother at dinner that night in the cafeteria. What did he think about for all those laps? What mental images was he ferrying back and forth across the pool? Was he continuing the train of thought he had shared earlier, meditating the nature of identity and fate? Could it be that, immersed in water, his mind looked no different than his younger brother's, a gray prism, scattering a spectrum of black and white?

On an impulse, Teddy turned to Fichter and asked, "What do you think about when you're swimming?"

In profile, Leo's eyes were as flat and calm as the surface of an empty pool. "I think about beating the guy next to me," he said.

Teddy elected not to set out for Leo the theory of consummation in either its original or its revised form.

To our right, which was the direction of Norm's office, metal scraped against tile as a chair was being pushed back from a desk. With two crouching steps, a suddenly furtive Leo Fichter was immersed in the nearest lane and pulling stroke-for-stroke with the sprinters.

Norm had come out with the purpose of unveiling the climactic set of the afternoon. For once, everybody would be doing the same thing—twenty fifties on forty seconds. This must have been a standard finale to Norm's workouts. His announcement was delivered after an ironic pause and received with knowing groans, not however by Teddy.

In Teddy, the ensuing thirteen minutes and twenty seconds inspired something like awe, which inclined him to think of the spectacle as awe-inspiring. Before his eyes the pool turned into a giant metronome. One wave after another of swimmers, perfectly spaced, pushed off the wall and swam two lengths of the pool, flipping their turns in virtual unison at the far end. They touched in thirty seconds and left again ten seconds later. Watching them was like taking the back off a clock or opening the hood of a car while the engine was running. The parts were interchangeable. Teddy knew, for instance, that both Chip and Leo were in the pool; but he couldn't distinguish either of them. The set's distance and interval, both short, were such that motion was continuous. There seemed no reason it should ever stop.

Through the haze of his reverie, Teddy was aware that the signs of the end of his brother's workout and the advent of his own were appearing around him. The high windows across the pool had gone black and reflected the pool murkily. (Dark was falling earlier these days.) A few parents, having driven their children in from some remote suburb, huddled in the bleachers, where they would sit for the duration of the following age-group workout. A distant din came from the locker room, but nothing could disturb the set in progress. The sound of splashing hands and feet rose from the water like a mist.

Rather than retreat again to his office, Norm Cohen took the seat beside Teddy on the bench so lately occupied by Chip and Leo Fichter in turn. Ted's conversation with Norm differed from the earlier two in that it was conducted entirely in silence. Nonetheless, he found this tete-a-tete the most flattering of the afternoon to date; and furthermore, it raised exactly the same question. What in the world was going through the mind of their coach? As the two of them sat unspeaking by the throbbing pool, Teddy glanced sidelong at the other's ruminating profile. It betrayed no hint of mental process. Could Norm Cohen have failed to harbor a trace of self-satisfaction that he had set all this in motion? Did it occur to him that a pool full of young men was willing, was avid to carry out any labor he could devise? What could they see in him, or for that matter what could they see in any human being that made them consent to daily suicide?

In fifteen minutes Teddy would be in their place.

CHAPTER TEN

Billy Wakes Up a Different Way

The Thursday of the following week witnessed the most natural, but (in fact) the least frequent permutation of our threesome. I drove down to swimming practice with my brother. This time, instead of going alone and early, I went with Billy and stayed late. There was going to be a clinic for high school coaches in the building that night, but swimmers of all ages were welcome, as Norm had smilingly told the team at the conclusion of the previous practice. A famous coach from another college would be speaking. There was something poignant about Norm's announcement. It was of the stoical kind issued by the teacher who informs her class that a Nobel Prize winner will be appearing that night in Oakland in the full knowledge that her students wouldn't walk as far as the water fountain to see this personage, if (in fact) the information even registered. But Billy not only noted Norm's invitation, he insisted we accept it.

On the way down to the pool, (for the sake of a complete survey, and also since conversation between my next older brother and me was often at a premium) I asked Billy what he thought about when he swam.

"I sometimes wish I was a distance swimmer, like Chip," he said, presumably in answer to my question.

He was looking straight ahead into the last of rush hour traffic on Washington Boulevard. By standing agreement he was driving down to practice, and I would drive back.

"Why?" I asked.

"For what you just said," Billy responded. "More time to think. Or rather more ways to think. The problem is, there is no standard 1500 yard swim. That would be the best distance, assuming a twenty-five yard pool."

"Why?" I asked again.

"Because that would be sixty lengths. That's divisible by a lot of prime numbers—two, three, five. With almost every length you would be completing some fraction of the total. It's fun to keep track while you're swimming. At least it's more fun than swimming." He paused. "It would be nice to have seven too, but by that time you'd be swimming the English Channel."

I turned and left Billy to his calculations. Naively, I had assumed his answer to the question would be less bizarre than Chip's.

On a Thursday, only nominally a school night in my view, we could afford to stay out later than usual. After our workout, with time to spare before the clinic started, Billy and I toured Trees Hall. As we worked our way from one wing of the building to the other, we gradually left the atmosphere of chlorine behind us and began instead to breathe in sweat and floor wax. In the gym upstairs, rubber chirped on hardwood. Around a corner the weight room clanked and wheezed like a boiler room.

The room we were looking for turned out to be one of several classrooms arranged around the building's central courtyard. It was surprisingly full. We found seats next to each other in a back corner. The audience consisted of both adults and children. Often a man and woman would flank a kid wearing a fleecy, patch-covered warm-up jacket over street clothes. The student desks proved somewhat snug on the men, and they wore the attached arms like a tool belt. Thus equipped, they sat slightly forward, vacantly alert, waiting for the clinic to begin. Up front (by a movie screen) sat a large, bespectacled man and a caricature of a collegian---a crew-cut, square-jawed young guy in a sport coat and tie. His build was also of the wide-shouldered variety. When he turned in his chair it was like a car door opening. Norm Cohen sat alongside, trading pleasantries with them.

Finally Norm stood up and introduced the older man as a swimming coach from a mid-western university and the author of a book. He referred to him familiarly as "Doc." The young guy was one of his swimmers and an alternate on the last Olympic team. His name was Don. Doc and Don.

Doc bellied up to the lectern. It was clear from the outset this was no pep talk. It was more like science class. Doc proved to be one of the least inspirational speakers by whom I had ever been addressed. His manner was slow and apologetic, almost sad. Comically, the room bristled with attention throughout his talk. "Swimming is applied physics," he began, and he went on to explain how in the water you had to consider basic mechanical principles like leverage and resistance, how for instance it was actually advantageous to pull with your fingers slightly apart. How you naturally lifted yourself out of a pool with bent rather than straight arms, and how this fact should be reflected in your stroke. The wings of a jet airplane entered into his theory at some point. Many people took notes.

Ten minutes into his talk his partner got up, walked over to the wall and turned out the lights. One row to my right, Norm Cohen manned a projector. Having dissolved into the shadows at the front of the room, Don reappeared in black-and-white on the screen, stripped to a tank suit and crouched on a starting block. He was still smiling pleasantly, but he seemed dreamy, or drugged, as he uncoiled stiffly into a racing dive. Then I realized that the film was in slow motion. There was no sound. In the very next frame, shot from below, Don shattered the surface of the water. He stretched to his full length, and then began what looked like an exotic dance, rhythmically waving his arms and legs. Or it could have been an appeal for rescue in pantomime. He would look to the side, open-mouthed with alarm, then straight ahead at us as though to speak. But only bubbles emerged from his mouth, like strings of pearls.

Before long, as these silent images and Doc's droning narration cast a spell over the room, I turned toward Billy to exchange some reaction and/or commiseration. But when I looked to my left I scarcely recognized my brother. He was wide-eyed, rapt, his face bathed in the flickering light of the projector. He might have been aglow himself. His mind was obviously on lifted elbows, not rational numbers. Failing to catch his eye, I turned back to the film, which at that moment, in a sudden square of white light and the whirring of an empty reel, concluded. When Doc solicited questions for himself and Don, a thicket of hands appeared in the air. We stayed for all of them.

As I drove home, Billy reviewed the presentation, studying the windshield as though it was still the movie screen. "Did you see the way his arms moved under water? The side view?" he said. "Did you know they bent like that?"

"That's what Norm always told us," I said. "That's what Chip does," I added; and I assumed this to be true even though I had never shot underwater footage of my brother's freestyle.

"I just didn't realize," Billy said.

From that night on Billy behaved differently. His life seemed to have an added dimension. I believe it is often referred to as "focus." He did calisthenics not only before he went to bed but also immediately after his first alarm went off, the period he had previously set aside for out-of-body, although still in-bed, experiences. The current issue of *Swimming World* appeared on the nightstand between our beds. The subscription order form inside the back cover was clipped out and presumably in the mail. He skipped that month's math club meeting in favor of practice. When I had a chance to observe him during workouts, I could tell that he was trying to implement Doc's theories. His elbows were higher on his recovery. His hands no longer crossed the vertical axis of his body when they entered the water, hence his characteristic shimmy disappeared.

The Tuesday before Thanksgiving, Norm Cohen staged a

time trial at the end of practice. It was one of those dark early winter days when dusk seems to arrive around noon in the form of low, smudgy clouds the color of graphite. Turnout for the age-group workout was light. However, since the bulk of Pitt's team had left early for Thanksgiving vacation, the college swimmers who lived too far away to go home for the long weekend and the locals like Chip joined us for a combined workout.

Time trials were always welcome, because they consumed a lot of clock. True, you had to bust a gut for, in this case, four lengths; but then you got to sit back and watch the exertions of your teammates at your leisure. Furthermore, on this occasion Norm set up numerous heats of no more than three or four swimmers, so we had all much longer to lounge on a bench or on the tile of the deck as we preferred. It was just coincidence, I assumed, that in the final heat of the day, Chip took the center lane flanked by his two brothers. I was on his left hand and Billy on his right. Norm had dismissed the other swimmers, so we had the vast natatorium to ourselves.

It was one of the most pleasant sprints I could remember. I stroked easily, but could tell I was going fast. I flipped my turns effortlessly. I didn't expect to beat Chip, and I didn't. But I kept his feet in sight for all four lengths to finish just over a body length behind him. The surprising thing was that when I looked past him I seemed to see a mirror image of myself. It was Billy, two lanes over, touching immediately after me. It was his best time by three seconds.

Norm Cohen stood over Billy's lane, gazing at his stopwatch. He looked shocked, possibly insulted by the time it recorded.

"What are you trying to do, Billy, beat your brothers?" he asked.

Inimitably, he then managed to make his next statement sound almost reproachful.

"You're getting in shape," he said.

CHAPTER ELEVEN

A Holiday Atmosphere

Thanksgiving morning, Teddy Livingstone woke up basted by pleasant and in some cases unfamiliar sensations. Above his head, the light that filtered through the curtains of his room, while of an indeterminate gray, was just lambent enough to suggest that he had slept late into a leaden November weekday. On the wall to his left, the higher, smaller window glowed dully like the screen of a television set with the sound turned down to a buzz. Already the smell of roasting turkey seeped along the floor like an invisible ground fog.

These phenomena were seasonal. The flush of his skin was not. It could be traced to the new electric blanket under which he basked. On many years Mrs. Livingstone gave her children a gift on some off-holiday, although usually Easter, usually things they "needed anyway." Teddy and his brothers had all received the same household good the night before as a Thanksgiving present. Strangest and most sobering of all Teddy's current feelings, however, was the solitude that settled over him. Billy's bed was empty.

On Teddy's way down the hall, Chip's dark, closed door contradicted all preceding evidence of an advanced hour. And he had taken no more than a few steps across the living room rug in his stocking feet when his mother stepped out of the kitchen with a finger to her lips. Mr. Livingstone, seated at the dining room table, met Teddy's eyes sternly as he turned a silent page of the newspaper and nodded in the same direction that his wife now pointed. Following their gazes, Teddy saw behind him an unprecedented sight. Chip was asleep on the living room couch. He wore his covers like a toga, one shoulder and one arm exposed as though in mid-gesture. He was frowning, either willing himself into oblivion or rebuking everyone else for being conscious.

Teddy drew two conclusions from the fact that Chip had slept longer than he had, and on a couch. First, there wasn't a swimming pool open anywhere in the tri-state area on Thanksgiving Day. Second, his girlfriend Susan was asleep in his bed. (Teddy had forgotten until this moment that Susan was visiting the Livingstones for part of the long weekend.) The fact that Teddy had slept longer than Billy was simply inexplicable, until he finally remembered Billy's calisthenics. Apparently they were scheduled for Thanksgiving the same as any other day. Teddy entered the kitchen to find Billy at the table eating a noiseless breakfast. At close range he could distinguish the smell of toast from that of turkey.

Just as I was finishing my own bowl of cereal, Chip got up from the couch. Although the day had now officially begun, for the next several hours things continued to happen in no particular order. First, Dad, Billy and I sat around the kitchen table as Chip and Susan ate their breakfasts. Mom stood at the stove simultaneously scrambling eggs for them and preparing creamed onions for dinner. As an audience we were all captivated, watching Susan pour orange juice for herself as though that was some novel California folkway. Chip produced a steady stream of stories about college and swimming, separately or in combination, as he took liberties with the condiments, scraping butter for his toast off the top of the stick, to the stupefaction of Susan in turn. Susan and Mom laughed at each other's jokes.

In the living room the television had come on, possibly spontaneously, to display a parade going on downtown. Our set was black-and-white rather than color, although on a day like the one outside it didn't make much difference. Different configurations of people lounged around and watched the parade idly. Occasionally, Mom sat down in her apron. At some point a football game came on the television set. I went down to Hooty's house for just an hour or so, forgetting that they ate their holiday dinners early—and often, and sometimes on days I hadn't realized were holidays. As I was wandering around the house on my return I came with a start across Billy doing homework in our room. I had tentatively set aside Sunday night for mine.

In the afternoon, two of Chip's friends stopped over to visit, J. T. Orum and Mike Howard. Both were swimmers who had gone away to different colleges in Ohio, one of them a good college and one mediocre college, although I couldn't remember which school was which. Each of them had a girl with him. Mom and Dad gave them a reception they must have rehearsed on V-E Day. (As Chip led his visitors into the game room they smiled and ducked their heads as though dodging ticker tape.) I took a chair in the living room near the door and pretended to read the newspaper Dad had discarded. In actuality, I was listening—not to the conversation, which I couldn't make out, but to Mike Howard's reaction to it, which was one of the greatest although all too infrequent pleasures of my life. His distinctive laugh operated on some sort of delay mechanism, beginning with a catch in his voice after he concluded a remark and then erupting into a deep, throaty guffaw that was filthier and funnier than any joke could possibly be.

It still seemed early when Chip's friends left, but when I

looked at the clock over the stove, I saw that school would have been out for a couple of hours. It was nearly dark outside.

This Thanksgiving we were hosting my mother's side of the family, consisting primarily of her sister, her sister's husband and their two children. They always arrived on the stroke of five o'clock, just early enough to make the interim before dinner awkward. On their heels, a pair of women appeared of whose relation to us I had never been sure. They were nobody's grandmother that I knew of, and they seemed too old to be anyone's cousins, except possibly each other's. They did however bake pies.

As my father heartily hung up everyone's coat, Wicky and Kim, my cousins, hovered by the front door with an air of polite confusion, as though they weren't convinced that this house was their final destination of the night. I recognized this expression as the one I wore when we visited their house. They attended a private boys' and girls' school, respectively, in a remote and alien suburb. Since they were both slightly younger than I, it was ultimately my responsibility to entertain them.

Underneath his camel hair topcoat Uncle Bob wore a coat and tie, and I suppose Aunt Helen's dress was correspondingly formal. Very shortly after he deposited his "wrap" with my father, Uncle Bob approached me with not one but both hands extended. I realized immediately that my uncle was not soliciting a secret handshake—in fact, I was apparently not yet of age for a standard handshake—much less a hug; but rather he was presenting me with my annual golf tip.

"Square-to-square, Teddy," he said. "That's what they're teaching these days."

Fitting his hands together in this revolutionary grip, he confided a swing or two in me.

When I explained to him again (kindly) that swimming was my sport (so kindly that my explanation glanced visibly off his bifocals) he said, "Sure, I like to jump in the pool after a hot round. But you know, a guy was telling me this the other day, and damn it, he's right when you think about it, that half your strokes are on the green. It stands to reason you should spend half your practice time putting."

Eventually, the kids were all sitting around one end of the living room carrying on a discussion of sorts over glasses of ginger ale that Chip had distributed. He was continually and cheerfully excusing himself to get something from the kitchen, as though he was oppressed by his duties and not shirking conversation. He and Susan ended up flanked by the two attentive brothers-in-law. Susan *did* play golf. She was *also* very pretty that night. Our bathroom smelled good.

On that score, the night before Susan arrived, Mom edged

past me as I was leaving the bathroom and gently closed the toilet, saying, "Many hostesses prefer to keep the lid down when not in use."

Mom smiled as though we were sharing a private joke without specifying that she belonged to this class of hostess. I assumed she did.

Anyone who concluded from the ensuing scene in the dining room that this family convened every year for the sake of a meal, Teddy reflected from his place at one end of the table, would be making a radical, understandable, mistake. There was certainly a great deal of food on hand. Holiday dinners in the Livingstone residence were always served buffet-style. In one corner of the room on a couple of card tables spread with tablecloths, one heaping plate after another surrounded the big yawning turkey carcass. Personally, Ted found the presence of certain of these dishes most profoundly reassuring, even if after sixteen Thanksgivings he had not yet sampled them. (Baked oysters belonged in this category.)

Actually, the true purpose of these gatherings was to pronounce a certain number of foreordained sentences. For instance, Mrs. Livingstone and her sister spent the whole evening establishing that their deepest mutual convictions had survived their latest separation. This confirmation took an oddly negative form. To each of her sister's assertions—"I don't think she ever intended to sell that house"—the other would respond with a resounding, slightly aghast "No," which really meant, "Yes, you're right, I agree with this view; and I always have agreed with it, and also with many others that you're not currently voicing, which is to be expected, as we're members of the same family. And that incidentally must be why we are all here tonight."

The remarks of Teddy's cousins, who were admittedly intelligent, had just the opposite implication. Kim, in particular, liked to deliver sweeping judgments unconnected with what had just been said and with anything that could possibly be said subsequently.

"I think folk rock is pointless," she might say in a conversation about school, and although Teddy had theretofore had no particular feelings one way or the other about that form of popular music, he felt a sudden taste for it come over him, as he suspected he was meant to have a sudden taste for it. Kim's every gesture implied that the Allen (Mrs. Livingstone's maiden name) blood line stopped with their parents, although Teddy, after his mother had traced the family tree for him in advance of the party, was in a position to explain to her that they were cousins removed not even once, as he had always assumed they were.

Of all the speakers present, Uncle Bob sounded much the most altruistic note. He seized every such occasion to bring his family (despite itself) abreast of the modern age.

"What about these engine housings, Chuck?" he might say to Mr. Livingstone on the subject of motorized vehicles, and in particular riding lawn mowers. "Everything's plastic these days. And car engines are so complicated. You can't find anything anymore. You're liable to reach for the dipstick and pull out a spark plug. But people are buying these big station wagons like they're going out of style."

Uncle Bob might more logically have said coming into style, but his point was clear. And while he directed these remarks to Teddy's father, he would try to catch other eyes, as though to alert his in-laws (without alarming them) to the rapid passage of the century. He managed throughout the meal to maintain his air of unheeded prophet.

But Teddy heeded him, if only to avoid talking to Kim and Wicky. The latter was a year or two younger than his sister, and quieter, although he seemed generally to endorse her opinions. Teddy also took advantage of the frequent gaps in his conversation with his cousins to observe his elder brother. He and Susan, although they sat only a couple of places away from Teddy, were firmly in the orbit of the adults. From the outset of the meal, it was clear that Chip would deliver his traditional performance. The minute the blessing had been pronounced, Chip got up from the table (as he never failed to do at a holiday dinner) to get one last buffet item, this time a scoop of stuffing directly from the carcass of the turkey rather than from the bowl that Mr. Livingstone had filled in the course of the carving. Having corrected his oversight, Chip seemed poised to dig in and eat. However, a full plate of food seemed to make him more talkative than hungry. He began to entertain everyone else while they ate with some of his finest anecdotes, largely about earlier family gatherings, many of which had taken place before Teddy was born, and therefore very likely before Chip was born. Nevertheless, to judge from the reception of these stories, his accuracy of detail was outstanding.

This year (once again) Teddy observed, a meal that he could attest had taken all day to prepare, was essentially concluded in ten minutes by everyone except Chip, undoubtedly because Chip had done so much talking. Long after the dinner was reduced to rubble, with shattered rolls and crumpled napkins lying around on the tablecloth, Chip sat before a steaming plate. Finally, as though coming to himself, he insisted everyone else begin dessert while he got a third helping of turkey.

"Chip may have brought a girl to a family dinner," Teddy thought, "but that doesn't mean all his habits have changed."

Over the next couple of days, however, he learned that some others had.

CHAPTER TWELVE

An Empty Couch

All day long I had been surprised how late it was. Then, when all my relatives rustled to their feet as one and stretched, flapped into their coats and dispersed at the front door like a flock of birds, I was surprised how early it was, barely ten. As I often did after a family function like this one, I wandered aimlessly around the house, starting with the kitchen, where Mom (with the help of Susan) was putting away the leftover food. Chip was already picking at the turkey that he had set down on a counter before he carried it out to the garage for the night. He always maintained, and I had to agree, that Thanksgiving dinner was really just a formality necessary to produce a carcass to maul for the next several days. Year in and year out, he was the one to salvage a last piece of stuffing from between two ribs of the turkey long after it had been declared exhausted. Dad paced the floor almost as idly as I, his host's smile frozen on his face as though to imply he could have gone another couple of hours. I ended up watching television in the living room, pleased to find the normal Thursday night programming on the air. (There was a deeper reality that holidays could not disturb.) Behind me, Mom made up the couch for Chip and announced, apparently for my benefit, that she was going to leave the dirty dishes for tomorrow. She and Dad retired, leaving me alone in the room.

When the news blared, I retreated to my own room. I found Billy already there, lying in bed with the covers pulled up to his chin. The lamp between our beds was lit, although no reading matter was in evidence.

"What are you doing?" I asked; and my tone sounded less friendly to me than I thought I had intended.

"Waiting for you," he said.

"I mean, what are you doing in bed so early?"

"There's a workout tomorrow, remember?"

"Oh," I said; I didn't. Then, as an afterthought, I asked, "Why are you waiting for me?"

"I wanted to talk to you," he said.

Perhaps it would not be strictly necessary that sentence be

followed by another, but I think it was only natural for me to expect one. In any case, Billy stopped. All his habits hadn't changed, either, even if he was now an early riser. As soon as he lay down, his syntax deteriorated. He began to speak in random, in scattered sentences, not that different from when he talked in his sleep. It was just a matter of degree.

"I wanted to talk to you about Chip," he said.

"Yes?"

"Do you like Susan?"

I laughed.

"What?" he questioned.

"I thought you wanted to talk about Chip."

"I do," he said. "Do you like her?"

"Yes," I said automatically, realizing that all along that question had probably been displaced in my mind by the question whether she liked me. "Do you?"

"I guess," I laughed again.

"I assumed you must have a strong opinion."

"Not really."

Once again, our conversation seemed at an end.

"Well?" I said. "What about Chip?"

"I have to show you something first," Billy said.

So Billy said, but then he lay still. By this time Teddy was also in bed, also on his back, and looking up at the ceiling, where their lamp, clicked to the lowest of its three wattages, cast its strange geometric shadow of light, a circle with a right angle where it folded into the corner of the room. After a minute, Teddy realized that his brother had not slipped into his usual interstellar sleep; rather, he was listening. So Teddy listened as well to the buzzing dusk of the house. And when Billy got out of bed, Teddy followed him. Like Billy, and Chip before him, Ted slept in his underpants, which in the murk of their room could be taken for a tank suit, the white, high-waist variety favored by divers. And in fact they tip-toed down the quivering hallway as though it were a board, stopping poised to spring and peering over its edge into the deep end of the living room. The atmosphere of the evening past hung over the room like a mist, the memory of food and cigarette smoke in the air was half smell, half taste. Amid the furniture, several metal TV trays remained snapped into place, full of glasses and their watery dregs. In front of the picture window, its sheets silvered by the single ray of moonlight that penetrated the curtains, Chip's makeshift bed sat like a shrine, an empty shrine.

Back in our room and in bed again, Billy said, "That's how it was this morning when I went down to the basement to do my sit-ups and pushups. Afterwards, I stopped in the kitchen and had something to drink. No one else was up yet. When I came back through the living room Chip was lying there asleep."

I absorbed this news in silence. Given the crypt-like quiet around me, there couldn't be much doubt that Chip was in the guest room along with the guest. He was a guest, too. It wasn't that I hadn't conceived the idea that Chip slept with Susan.

"They're not necessarily doing anything," I said. "You and Debbie used to swim naked together and not do anything, according to her."

"I wouldn't say 'anything,'" Billy said.

"Well, not everything."

Another pause ensued.

"He's different," Billy said. "They're not going to practice tomorrow. He told me."

"Is that what's bothering you?"

"I don't really think so," Billy said quizzically. "There's something else about him lately I'm not sure I like."

"What?"

"He seems happy."

As Teddy drifted off to sleep, he wasn't sure if it was that possibility or the thought that Billy's bed would be empty when he woke up that troubled him.

CHAPTER THIRTEEN

My Mother Gives Her Opinion of Soap Operas

Teddy's premonition was not exactly realized. In the gray early morning he turned over in his sleep to see Billy's outline under his covers like a familiar coastline. The next time he opened his eyes Billy was sitting fully dressed on his bed asking him if he wanted to go to swimming practice after all. To his own surprise, Teddy agreed. What followed was that rarity, a refreshingly grueling workout. On the day after Thanksgiving Trees Hall was deserted. Ted and Billy walked past the locked office doors of blank linoleum hallways to the men's locker room. It was another combined practice, again with more age-group than college kids.

As Teddy and Billy headed for the showers after their last fifty, Norm said, "And tell your brother to get the hell down here once in a while."

He was a master of mild profanity.

By early afternoon, after the turkey had been set out and systematically worked over by everyone, our family dispersed. Dad had been at work all day. Billy took the other car on condition he do some errands for Mom. Chip went with Susan into his room to help her pack and straighten up things. She was going to be picked up by a girlfriend and spend the rest of the weekend at her house. I retreated to my room with the view eventually of going down to Hooty's. So far as I knew, the day after Thanksgiving was not observed as a holiday in the Hurwitz household. After reading on my bed for a while, I got up and started down the hall. The house was to all appearances empty.

But then I heard the sound of voices in the living room. I walked in to find Mom in her typical television-viewing posture, sitting on the arm of an easy chair with a dish towel dangling from one hand. The expression on her face, a mixture of amusement and bafflement, went along with the posture.

"Honestly," she said, presumably to me, although her eyes never left the screen, "who watches these soap operas? Let alone believes them? The characters are always asking one another, 'Are you all right?' Of course they're not all right! Why else do they stammer when they say, 'Oh, I'm fine?'"

Teddy had to concede his mother did a pretty fair imitation of an anguished soap opera heroine.

"Ninny," she went on apostrophizing the television set. "If you would just wait a minute while the camera pulls in for a close-up of her face you would see that she's not fine. Well, who would be when they just found out the gardener at their house is really their father?"

Having delivered this critique, my mother moved around and sat down on the edge of the chair, seemingly more sad than angry. I half-reclined on the couch, my elbow sinking into Chip's bedclothes, which still lay there in a heap, and watched along with her. She was absolutely right. At that very moment a woman's twitching face filled the screen, while over her shoulder a man continued (unsuspecting) to fix himself a drink. When a commercial began Mom and I talked. For the fiftieth time I asked her, and she explained to me, how the two women at dinner the night before were related to each other and to me. (I knew it was a subject she never found boring.)

Then the strangest thing happened. Still bemused, Mom began to twist the dish towel in her hands. This was a new mannerism in her repertoire. At first, I assumed the soap opera must be nearing still another climax. I had stopped listening. But another commercial was on TV. At that moment I realized, or rather sensed, that the house was even less empty than I had supposed. Chip and

Susan had never come out of his room. Something else did instead. Like a specter, Sex walked straight through the closed (if not locked) door of Chip's bedroom and into the living room where it sat down cross-legged on the floor between Mom and me. It wasn't watching the television. It was watching us. Then it puffed itself up slowly like a bullfrog, swelling until it burst (albeit invisibly) into a suffocating vapor with an odor both too embarrassing and too obvious on which to comment. Without saying a word to each other, Mom and I both knew that Chip and Susan had (as of that second) been in his room too long. They were doing something, and it wasn't a set of two one-hundreds.

"He certainly spends a lot of time in her bedroom," Mom said with the same half-distracted, half-amused smile that the soap opera had provoked from her—or was continuing to provoke, since she was still watching it. "If he was my daughter I know I'd have him out of there in a hurry. I mean, if *she* was my daughter. Well, you know what I mean."

"I know," I said.

"Oh, enough of this nonsense," Mom said, standing up. "I'll turn it on a week from now, and I won't have missed a thing. But maybe I can get those dishes done by then."

As I made for the front door, Mom disappeared into the kitchen. The television was still running.

CHAPTER FOURTEEN

Am I My Brother's Coach?

I got back from Hooty's just before dinner. In my absence the house had apparently been exorcised of all spirits. Sex was no longer in the air, and the smell of cigarette smoke had finally dissipated. On opposite easy chairs, Chip and my father sat talking in the living room. Their subject was Susan, who had been picked up by her friend.

"Nice girl," Dad said. "Let's get Teddy one just like her."

"He has Cindy," Chip said.

"Oh, sure. I wasn't thinking," Dad said. "Is that where you were just now?"

"Her family went to Florida for the week," I explained.

"I knew that," Dad said.

Perfectly plausibly, Chip said, "Why don't you fly us to Florida for Thanksgiving next year, Dad?"

Dad gave him a look.

Cindy wouldn't be back in class until a week from Monday. She was identifiable on sight as one of those students who got extra school days off for travel.

Dinner that night was essentially a reenactment of the previous night's, minus the relatives and the silverware. Over the next few days, one side dish after another would disappear from the buffet, until only the carcass was left. The Livingstone family's ability to stretch a turkey was limited only by Mrs. Livingstone's willingness to make extra stuffing. Neither her husband nor her sons voiced the stereotypical complaints over Thanksgiving left-overs. Here again, they very likely followed as a group the eldest son's lead. The more remote the turkey by-product, the more heartily Chip welcomed it.

Teddy Livingstone traditionally spent the Friday night of a Thanksgiving weekend at home savoring his insulation from school by a day on one side and two days on the other. The night in its passage would tip the balance. Of course, with Cindy away he had no compelling alternative this year. His parents were out at a party, and he and his brothers had tacitly dispersed through the house. Midway through the evening, as though scheduled to patrol the grounds, Teddy got up from the newspaper he had been reading at the kitchen table. He stepped over his brother Billy (who was watching television prone on the living room carpet) on his way to the bedrooms. He found Chip moving around his room like a shopkeeper straightening up before opening. He ran his fingertips along the spines of some books on a shelf. Teddy entered the room like the first customer of the day. As he pushed the door the rest of the way open, he wouldn't have been surprised to hear a chime.

"Hi," he said.

"Hi," Chip said.

"You haven't done any homework since you've been home," Teddy said, dropping into the chair by the door.

Chip looked around with an air of mock-disorientation and said, "I'll have it on your desk tomorrow morning."

"I didn't mean it like that," Ted laughed, as much at the ease he had instantly achieved in Chip's easy chair as at his remark. "It just struck me this second," Ted told him.

"I'm going back early on Sunday," Chip said. "I'll have all day and all night. The library stays open until midnight on Sunday."

"On Sunday?"

"It closes early on Friday and Saturday nights, you know; because those are party nights. It closes at five o'clock, I think, maybe six. It might have been closed this Friday and Saturday. I'm

not sure."

"What about practice?" Ted asked.

"What about it?"

Chip lay down on his back on his bare mattress, which Mom had stripped of the sheets Susan used, and had not yet remade. Flesh-colored and dented with buttons like so many navels, the mattress could have been a mutant torso. With a diver's half-twist, Chip reached up and behind him to punch a cover-less pillow into shape and set it under his head.

"Are you going tomorrow?" Teddy asked. "Norm asked about you this morning."

"Norm's a good man," Chip mused. "He's a good man and a great coach. Or maybe that's vice versa. The divers weren't practicing today. I thought I should be a good host and stay here with Susan. I'll go tomorrow."

"Fichter wasn't there either."

"Fichter may have a family," Chip said. "They may celebrate Thanksgiving. In which case, they probably have turkey."

"Creamed onions," Teddy said.

"Frightening."

"But I doubt whether he gives your home life much thought."

"You're probably right."

To his brother's surprise, Chip laid his head back on the

pillow in silence. Teddy naturally expected a theory to follow and a comment upon their last exchange, but apparently Chip did not have one prepared for every occasion. And when Teddy spoke again, Chip opened his eyes as though after a long sleep.

"I guess what I'm getting at is, will you be ready for the Christmas meet?

The subject that Teddy was rather formally raising was the big AAU swimming meet that took place every year between Christmas and New Year's at Trees Pool. Age-group teams from all over the city, even from neighboring states, competed.

"I'm not worried so much about the Christmas meet," Chip said. "I think of myself as a college swimmer now."

"You should worry about it, Chip," Teddy said. "It's a chance to prove yourself to Norm."

In the space of the couple of months that he had swum for Norm's AAU club, Teddy had developed a certain indulgence toward his teammates. He could not in all objectivity characterize the behavior he witnessed every day after practice in the shower and locker room of Trees Hall as anything other than psychopathic. In no other social context that he had experienced would a guy next to you, naked and soaping his groin, look you directly in the eye and break into the chorus of a top forty tune in falsetto. The shrieks and whistles turned the shower room into a steamy tile aviary. Outside by their lockers guys in underpants wrestled and snapped towels at each other. They told infantile jokes, but Teddy reasoned when young adults spent hours on end swimming around in circles as their peers were socializing on dry land, you might expect their personalities to regress.

Only on the subject of competitive swimming were Teddy's teammates coherent, and the Christmas meet had been a topic of locker room conversation virtually from the first practice of the fall. Winning times from years past, with legendary names attached to them, were quoted to the tenth of a second. Chip had swum for Norm only for a few years. Some of the kids on the team had entered the meet (seemingly) since infancy. Teddy gathered that college swimmers were not eligible as such. They could, however, represent their AAU club in the "open male" age group, using the meet as a tune-up for the college swimming season that began in earnest when school started again early in the new year.

"See," Teddy went on, "if you don't beat Fichter in the Christmas meet, you may have no college swimming career. And you told me that was what you wanted. You told me that."

Teddy had the further impression that Norm Cohen occasionally treated the Christmas meet as a trial to decide who would swim for him in Pitt's first college meets. Some of his non-local swimmers came back immediately after Christmas just to swim in the meet. And unless he erred, Chip was the source of this impression.

At the moment, Chip remained on his back on the bed tossing a tennis ball in the air. Teddy knew the game. You tried to throw the ball as close as possible to the ceiling without touching it. (The problem was being sure you couldn't always get the ball just one micron closer.)

"Do you realize you have a way of looking beyond meets?" Teddy said. "This past summer you couldn't concentrate on Community's meets, and it was the AAU meets that really mattered. But you had to beat Progar, who swam for Chapel Gate and not for an AAU club. You had to beat Progar at the Chapel Gate meets and at the championships, but what counted was that Community won the team title. If you were entered in a sprint, you were really a distance swimmer. You always focused on some farther goal. Now you're obsessed with Fichter. You beat him in workouts. Every single day, every single set, I see you do it. Now you have to beat him in a meet, this meet."

Teddy could not have said at what point he became aware that he was lecturing his brother. Perhaps it was when he found himself pacing the floor at the foot of Chip's bed. Perhaps it was when he noted the amusement on Chip's face as he said, "Thank you, Doc Livingstone."

Teddy stopped in his tracks, sobered by this allusion to the coach whose clinic he and Billy had attended that night after practice. He sat back down in the easy chair.

"That guy was interesting," he said.

"He certainly found a disciple in Billy," Chip said.

"You know," Teddy said, "you used to criticize Billy for not dedicating himself to swimming."

". . . or to anything else, for that matter."

"Well, lately he has. And he's good at other things. But you still belittle him."

"I do?"

"Not exactly in words."

"By my existence?"

"Why can't you take him seriously?"

"I've wondered about that."

As he was answering his brother's charges, Chip got into a groove with the tennis ball. One flight after another nearly grazed the ceiling, but not quite. Then he caught the ball and held it on his chest.

Teddy had concluded long since that it was difficult, if not redundant, to make a funny person laugh. He arrived at this general truth by extrapolating from his relationship with his eldest brother. He had never really figured out why Chip liked him, as he genuinely seemed to, when he could not be amused by him. If Chip did laugh when Teddy said something, it was more because it was something Chip might have said. And then Teddy laughed as well at the implied imitation. They both laughed.

Not only was it hard to amuse a source of one-liners, it was hard to criticize one. But additionally, it was hard to criticize Chip because he was basically thoughtful. For all his quips, and thinking two sentences ahead in a given conversation, he listened to everything you said. His memory was phenomenal. He might ask you what you meant by a chance remark you had made a month ago. In a conversation like the present one, just when you thought you hadn't gotten through to him, you were afraid you might have hurt him. His face clouded over.

"I guess it's just sort of unthinkable that your next youngest brother could beat you at something," Chip mused. "It seems unnatural. Somehow it wouldn't be so bad if it was the youngest brother. You'd be proud of him. He would be a prodigy. It would be funny that he had beaten you, but not in an embarrassing way. And, in this particular case, you are faster than Billy." He paused. "Is that what you came in here to tell me?"

"What?" Teddy asked.

At this juncture, T. C., their cat, walked into the room. She jumped up and sat on Chip's desk, blinking slowly first at one of them and then at the other, as though moderating their discussion. Teddy realized he hadn't seen her all weekend.

"You've touched on a number of topics tonight," Chip said, "but is what you've been trying to break to me all along that you're going to beat me in the Christmas meet?"

"That's impossible," Teddy said, with something like disdain, although he was its only possible object.

"Why?" Chip said.

"We're not even in the same age group. Whereas, Billy has actually turned eighteen."

"Sometimes Norm swims younger guys in the open male division," Chip said, "for experience. You're allowed to go up an age group as long as you make the qualifying time."

"You have to qualify for the Christmas meet?"

"For the open division," Chip said. "You just have to show that you swam below the cut-off time for your event in some meet with official timers," he said as he reached under his nightstand and pulled out a book, which he tossed over to Teddy. "It's all there in black and white."

Teddy found himself leafing through one of those official looking paperbacks with the canvas-like covers, now ragged and bleached. Apparently chlorine got to books, too. This was a swimming rulebook put out by some association.

"Well, maybe so," Teddy said; "but there's another reason I couldn't beat you."

"What is that?"

"You're better than I am."

"So?" Chip asked.

He began to toss the ball again, but apparently by different rules. Now it was a game of reflexes. He bounced the ball off the ceiling, lightly at first, then harder, catching it first with one hand and then with the other.

"You're saying that you still know your place?" he asked.

"That's it," Teddy said.

"Well."

As Chip spoke, he reached for the tennis ball, which had taken a funny bounce off the ceiling, perhaps under the influence of a spin, and missed. The ball rolled under his desk on the far side of the room. T. C. bolted through the door into the hall. Chip's open left hand remained extended out over the edge of the bed. He closed his eyes.

"Well, I will give your remarks careful consideration. Now, make my bed without moving me."

He opened his eyes.

"I'm Just kidding. Mom should be home soon."

CHAPTER FIFTEEN

Descent Into Pain

The comic menace of Norm Cohen was not always that comic.

When Teddy walked into Trees Pool at the head of his family contingent that Saturday morning, his coach greeted him pleasantly enough. Since he and his brothers were a little early, Teddy volunteered on their behalf to help put up the lane markers. Chip went over to the far side of the pool to unwind the blue-and-gold plastic ropes from their massive spools. Billy dropped into the water to swim each one across the pool. Because turnout would be light again, they skipped the lane marker that ran under the one-meter board so that the divers could practice when they arrived. While

Teddy hooked each line into place, Norm kneeled beside him with a wrench to tighten it. Throughout this process, Teddy rattled away about topics he assumed were of mutual interest to them, such as whether it was indeed possible for swimmers to move up an age group at the Christmas meet, given of course the proper qualifying time. Of course, he already knew this to be the case from his perusal of the rulebook Chip had given him.

There was a line from Hamlet, which under the direction of Mr. Hudak Teddy's English class had read earlier in the fall, describing the protagonist's disconcerting reticence. One of Hamlet's old friends, either Rosencrantz or Guildenstern, reported him to the king as "niggard of question, but of our demands most free in his reply." Teddy loved the sound of the line (not to mention the names of the characters) and once he had ascertained that it did not contain a racial slur, he was always on the lookout for melancholics to whom it would apply. Uncharacteristically, the line fit Norm that morning. While he replied to all Teddy's demands quite freely, Teddy imagined that Norm fetched his responses up with something between a sigh and a groan, and he lapsed into silence after each one—although perhaps that much was simply characteristic. His laugh failed inappropriately to boom. Teddy's first reaction was to wonder if even swimming coaches occasionally got sick of swimming. Maybe Norm would have liked to discuss the economies of developing nations. Second, without being able to shut himself up, and with some dismay, Teddy listened to himself turn into one of those kids like his teammate Gaffney at Community Swim Club who appointed themselves assistant coaches. He began to look forward to the start of practice and the immersion of his mouth.

When we finally lined up for practice, it worked out that there were just three or four swimmers per lane. Chip, Billy and I had one to ourselves. Fichter was present, although several lanes away from us.

A Norm Cohen signature workout soon took shape. Norm loved to start us out with short stuff—fifties, seventy-fives—and then move on to long, grueling sets. These first laps never seemed to add up to anything. You'd think you had been swimming forever, only to realize you hadn't yet gotten your first thousand completed.

That day we began with fifties. Norm sat impassively in his poolside folding chair and divulged one set at a time to his expectant swimmers.

"Ten fifties on a minute" was the sum and substance of his first pronouncement.

When we surfaced after this set, he uttered only the following slightly varied few syllables: "Ten fifties on fifty-five." His terseness was not unprecedented, but something else in his delivery was different—whether it was a smaller-than-usual diameter of his nostrils, so often flared with irony, or a more stolid set of the jaw. In either case, an unmistakable pattern was emerging. We were going to keep swimming sets of ten fifties—a total of twenty lengths, two at a time—while decreasing the space between them by five seconds per set. In other words, we were going to get progressively less rest between fifties. Therefore, it came as no surprise when Norm next specified ten fifties on fifty seconds. He could, without violating any articles of the Geneva Convention, take the present group down to an interval of forty seconds. And he did.

The sigh of relief that greeted the last of the fifties proved in retrospect to be a rather foolish one.

The set that followed immediately was not so bad, a round of kicking and pulling. Like insolent waiters, my teammates slouched back from the equipment room holding their kickboards out in front of them like Styrofoam trays with a pull-buoy balanced on top. This interlude was more tedious than tiring, however. With our heads out of the water while we kicked, we all seemed to scent the prospect of a long, tough set in the air.

The set arrived as forecast: ten two hundreds, on an interval such that you just had time after each eight-length sprint to draw a deep breath, bring your eyes into focus on the pace clock, and set off on the next. Chip, who led our lane, just seemed to get stronger as the set progressed. As the third and final swimmer in our circle, it was all I could do toward the end to keep from getting caught by Chip coming up from behind me. With every breath my lungs flared like the tips of two cigarettes. My retinas ached.

When this set ended, swimmers draped themselves over the lane markers as though on the floating spars of a wrecked ship.

Norm sat in his folding chair.

The set that Norm announced as the day's last sounded innocuous: four fifties on a minute. We had done fifty fifties, mostly on a shorter interval, to open the workout. These final four fifties amounted only to a single two hundred, of which we had just done ten. However, Norm's command contained the dreaded postscript: "Descend."

The object of a descending set was twofold, to swim each fifty faster than the one before and to collapse one or more lung on the final fifty.

Each lane would swim as a separate heat. Lane eight—Chip, Billy and I—would go last. As the first few swimmers took their marks along the wall, some of their teammates left to await their turns at the final set. (Fichter swaggered toward the showers, from which a steamy hiss could soon be heard. Leo, as always, made straight for the last shower on the wall, turning on all the others full blast on the way. Chip got in the shallow end of the pool to stay loose. He stroked across the empty expanse like a solitary swimmer in a sylvan lake. Billy and I were content to sit on a bench as spectators of the early heats.)

Hefting his most ornate stopwatch, Norm started the first group, then shouted out their times as they touched after each fifty. When they were finished, the swimmers had to recite their splits one by one. They had all managed to descend, or said they did. Norm waved them out of the pool.

Some fifteen minutes later, Norm convened the final heat. As it worked out it included not only the three Livingstone brothers but also Leo Fichter, who emerged at just that point from the locker room, windmilling his arms, snapping rather than stepping with his feet. He may finally have achieved the looseness for which he longed. (At least he seemed to have developed a couple of additional joints in the course of his shower.) He and Chip claimed the center lanes, as was only right. Billy and I flanked them. We all hung on the gutter and waited for the start.

What followed was a blur of pain. After the first fifty (which I stroked easily and with a clear conscience since we were supposed to start this set slow) every subsequent length was a separate, spoon-sized taste of death. Each time I touched at the end of a fifty, I snapped my head out of the water, first for air and then to hear my time, which was the last announced by Norm. It followed that no one touched after me. I knew that Fichter, just to my right, was beating me; I had a fine view of his receding feet. But three lanes away Billy must be beating me too! At the set's conclusion, as the last finisher, I reported my splits first. At least I had descended, if only by a few tenths of a second at a time. Billy had descended, too, a little more impressively; and Fichter was way ahead of both of us. Jack called Chip's name last. Therefore, he had beaten Fichter.

"My times came down, I'm pretty sure," Chip said.

"I didn't ask for an estimate," Norm said. "What were your splits?"

"About the same as Leo's, I guess," Chip said, still panting. "Maybe a tenth or two faster each time."

"You're not hearing me," Norm said. "I asked what your splits were. This is no time for modesty. The point is to get your times in your head so you can pace yourself. You have to know exactly how fast you're swimming. What were your times?"

"Actually," Chip said, "I prefer not to know my times in practice."

Before Teddy saw Norm's do it, he had not realized that a face could blush black.

"You'd prefer not to know your times?" Norm exploded. "Then what am I walking around here for pushing these little buttons on this watch and screaming at the top of my lungs? My health?"

I don't know if Norm intended to throw his pipe in the pool or if it just slipped out of his gesticulating left hand, the one that wasn't weighted down with the stopwatch. The pipe skipped off the deck and into the lane next to me. With as little motion as possible I fished it out of the water and set it on the tile.

"No one here cares what you prefer."

Norm really was screaming now, into a cavernous quiet. Only when a springboard stops twanging every ten seconds do you realize that it has been ringing in your inner ear for the past hour as divers paraded off it. But the silence that followed was ugly rather than soothing. Everyone in the building stood stock-still, with the partial exception of Susan, who sat on the end of the board, dangling her brown legs over the water, bobbing. Apparently, I was not the only person present hearing a tirade from Norm for the first time, and the first tirade of which to my knowledge my eldest brother had ever been the object.

"Unless, would you prefer not to swim for Pitt?"

Evidently the question was not rhetorical, because Norm repeated it.

"I said, would you prefer not to swim for me?"

We all waited for Chip to answer. He hung on the side of the pool, his head bent, the water lapping at his mouth.

"No one cares if you win a set in practice," Norm said. "The object of a set is not to win it, anyway. It's to see that its purpose is served. And no one cares if you beat Leo Fichter here. You have to do it in a meet, like at the Christmas meet. I have to see who can help me. Leo can swim any number of events. But if you want to swim for me, you'll have to swim the two hundred. Now, do you want to swim for me?"

"Yes," Chip said.

"Then do the set again," Norm said. "And this time remember your splits. Descend your fifties, and everyone goes home. Don't, and everyone swims a backwards eight hundred IM, courtesy of Chip Livingstone."

Sometimes the comic menace of Norm Cohen was not comic, and it wasn't funny, either.

Watching Chip repeat that descending set was more painful than any swim we might have to do afterwards as punishment could have been. As soon as Norm stopped talking, the divers, led by Susan, filed into the locker room, possibly out of compassion but more likely because all divers are prima donnas by nature. The rest of the team thronged the deck, urging Chip on in his humiliation. Even the phlegmatic Leo Fichter, no man to swim any more laps than absolutely necessary, showed a surge of team spirit. But after the first fifty, which Chip took out commendably, but unrealistically fast if he expected to descend, the cheers of his teammates were polite at best. You could watch Chip lose heart virtually in mid-stroke. He may have swum the second fifty slightly faster than the first, but the third fifty was appreciably slower, and he limped home with a 35.2. He quoted all his times for Norm to the self-incriminating tenth of a second, not that the backwards eight hundred IM wasn't painful.

CHAPTER SIXTEEN

Slow Dance

The following Saturday night, Teddy was taking Cindy to the dance at the Fox Chapel Presbyterian Church. Although it took place in only the first weekend of December, this affair was billed as the Christmas Dance. Starting the day after Thanksgiving, it seemed that every event was Christmas-related—parties, swimming meets. Teddy was getting as disgusted with this trend as his mother was, who annually reported her first sighting of a Christmas display at a store in the shopping center. Teddy's current position on Christmas was the following: see that he got a present and/or out of school, and you were entitled to associate your product with the holiday, but not otherwise.

After swimming practice on the Saturday of the dance, Teddy had the house pretty much to himself. Billy stayed in Oakland after their workout for some special all-day math test being given for district high school students on the campus of Pitt; and his parents were down at the shopping center—his mother presumably to expose and denounce premature Christmas sales. They were going to pick Billy up after his test. Teddy ate a late and leisurely lunch and then tried to do some homework. Unjustly, assignments always took longer if you did them in advance. In between math problems he flipped the dial of their television set. Reception was good that day, and he picked up the ghostly out-of-state station on channel nine. Watching it was like attending a séance. He tuned in The Wide World of Sports *in the hope they might have on some swimming, which they did once or twice a year, although they always coupled it with another, equally obscure sport, cutting away in the middle of the longer freestyle events to a European car race or a fencing championship. The swimming meets they did show were invariably held on snowy New England college campuses, one of which Billy might end up at in a year's time. Sooner than that, in eight months, Teddy would be a brotherless child. As he got dressed for the dance, he watched the first couple of bouts on* Studio Wrestling. *He would have to miss the headline Texas death match.*

From the moment he left his house, Teddy could not shake the feeling he was about to pick up Cindy for a first date, whereas they had been going out more or less steadily since summertime. Maybe this sensation was the effect of the unforeseen solitude he had enjoyed all day. That night he had the station wagon, since Billy wasn't going to the dance or anywhere else. Then Cindy's parents met him at the door of their house, the first time they had ever greeted him jointly. Finally, Cindy was scarcely recognizable; or rather, she had recaptured an earlier self, somehow acquiring during her week in Florida the same deep, tropical tan she had during the summer. He might be viewing her again from the terrace of Community Swim Club.

It was Cindy's first church dance since she had moved into the area. Held four or five times a year, these social events seemed an institution in themselves to Teddy's circle of friends. As always, adult chaperons stood around the vestibule while admission was being paid and hands were stamped. They smirked benignly by way of implying they knew how to have a good time, as though their coats and ties didn't announce the opposite. One wing of the church was open for the evening. The dance took place straight ahead in what (on other occasions) passed for a gym. There were backboards and hoops on the walls, but there was a stage at one end of the room; and the floor was linoleum tile. Restrooms and water fountains were available outside in whitewashed halls that retained the slightly medicinal smell of Sunday school. Only Teddy and the few of his fellow church members among the revelers could sense the empty sanctuary at the other end of the building. He imagined if someone inadvertently opened the doors onto that vacuum, all the dancers might be sucked out of the gym and into the pews like passengers out of a breached jet airplane.

While the band, of which Hooty was a member, set up, Cindy and Teddy socialized separately and as a couple. More girls than guys flocked around Cindy; and predictions about how long her tan would last were made. The regular cast of Teddy's friends was on hand. Mark Palmer appeared in one of his patented pastel-color crew-neck sweaters, this one a bright maroon on the brink of the effeminate. One of these times his sweater was going to match his date's, and then he would learn the meaning of the word "grief." Bill Burnley let it be known that outside under the front seat of his car he had secreted a bottle of Vat 69, which would serve as a source of both alcohol and double entendres all night long.

Even when the music started Teddy was in no hurry to get out on the floor. He was not a bad dancer, and Ted had no immediate plans to audition for American Bandstand; *but he also would never embarrass neither himself nor his partner during a standard number. Nevertheless, he and Cindy passed the first set in conversation with various people; and at the break he took her up to visit Hooty over a Dixie cup of the pineapple juice offered as refreshment for any social function at his church and every other church Teddy had ever attended. After a quick stretch, Hooty sat back down to talk from behind the electric organ that represented his life savings as well as several deferred birthday presents and made him sought after by every band in the area. The other members of this particular group went to Shady Side Academy, the private school nearby the church. For performances, they favored army field jackets worn over oxford cloth shirts.*

After the break, the dancing began in good earnest. Not surprisingly, although Teddy had not known this, Cindy was a superb dancer. With her hands sculling at her waist as though treading air, she simultaneously smiled and shrugged in a way that it would be a disservice to call a move. The crowd both on and around the dance floor was growing. You came to expect contact with random hips. People were still arriving, including some people Teddy knew went to college locally, and not just the hangers-on who showed up at all the high school's home football games and did everything but report to homeroom the year after they graduated. It wasn't inconceivable that Chip would show up here. Well, it was. Teddy hadn't seen or spoken to him since the disastrous practice the past Saturday morning.

Mike Guthrie, however, a couple of years and eighty pounds Chip's senior, strode onto the floor at just that moment and made up for lost time. Heading straight for the foot of the stage, with two consecutive steps he kicked off his loafers—by preference rather than church policy—and danced for a good thirty seconds by himself before his date could join him. Early in the number Mike twirled his index fingers at belt level, first off one hip and then the other, in the manner of a reel letting out line. It was by no means an original move, but it was well executed. Although Teddy would have classified the current song as a fast dance, Mark Palmer held his date in his arms—or rather in his "harms," as Hooty correctly pointed out the word was pronounced on the record.

Teddy and Cindy spent the better part of the second break outside leaning against the low brick wall, topped with a low hedge, that ran the length of the sidewalk to the parking lot. After their exertions in the gym, it was pleasant to stand without their coats in the cold night air under a sky so clear and sharp it had corners. Single stars shone faintly, as though each embedded in its own facet of the sky and seen from the side. The church lawns were singed white with frost.

If the early evening had felt to Teddy like a first date, its next phase was suddenly his wedding night. The band's third and final set consisted largely of slow numbers. Somehow, during the slowest of them, Teddy and Cindy ended up at the center of the dance floor. His cheek pressed against Cindy's, his face grazed by her hair, Teddy watched the other dancers spin slowly around them as though on a revolving stage. Everyone seemed entranced, although some of Teddy's friends' closed eyes seemed more obligatory than the others. On the stage, amid the plumes of chords he sent from his amp, Hooty sat impassively behind the sunglasses he wore even indoors when he played. Once as Teddy turned, his stare was riveted by that of Debbie's (Billy's old girlfriend) from over the shoulder of someone other than Billy. Her gaze was as meaningful as ever. Suddenly, Tommy Ludwig glided through Teddy's field of vision, winking and holding up his circled thumb and index finger in the OK sign, as though Teddy had assumed his relationship with Cindy was common knowledge. The real surprise would be if Tommy ever showed up with a date. Admission to the dance would be declared free that night.

As he more or less narrated all this to Cindy, who after all must be or at least could be seeing much the same thing over his shoulder, Teddy could feel rather than hear her laugh. She shuddered softly against him. She slipped her hand out of his and laid it with her other around his neck.

When the music stopped and the lights came up punctually at ten-thirty, Teddy's time-lapse night continued. In the parking lot, as dates were seated in cars and drivers exchanged farewells over the roar of engines, it occurred to him that car doors could be slammed surprisingly expressively. He then drove Cindy not to the site of their honeymoon, as he would have had the church dance really been their wedding reception, but right into the middle of a long suburban marriage. Cindy's parents had gone out; and a baby sitter, a ninth grader and next-door neighbor, met Teddy and Cindy at the Floods' front door. Cindy found one of her mother's pocketbooks and paid the girl. When the door had shut behind her, Teddy said, "Check on the kids, would you, dear?"

Cindy smirked back at him from the stairs, but in fact she did look into her sister's bedroom. When she came out, she beckoned to Teddy from the landing, and he followed her down the hallway to her room.

As they lay on Cindy's bed and kissed, an image entered Teddy's mind. It was not all that unusual in such a situation, with a vision already in front of him, for his brain to put on its own separate slide show. Its setting was often Chip's room. This time the first exhibit was another of the cartoons from the New Yorker *album that his brother kept by his bed. In it, an old-time bartender stood under a large oil portrait of a voluptuously, ridiculously naked woman. He said to his customer, "It's a painting of which we've never grown tired." For Teddy to ease Cindy's blouse out of her shorts or skirt and rest his hand on the cool small of her back at some point during a date had become almost routine, but it was a routine of which he had yet to grow tired.*

On this their wedding night or silver anniversary or whatever special occasion it was, he felt entitled to do something else. No, he felt called on to do something else. The question was what? Or where? Cindy was wearing a heavy, high-necked sweater that he couldn't imagine removing. In fact, he wasn't sure how it could be put on in the first place. Out of a half-open eye he examined a system of thongs and oblong buttons at the collar that might or might not have been functional. He stepped his fingers along Cindy's spine but met solid fabric. He felt as though he was groping in a laundry bag for a clean sock.

All he thought he was doing next was shifting his weight on the bed. He jammed his hand between Cindy's hip and the mattress for leverage but in the process pulled her closer to him as though trying to wind one of his legs between hers, which also was not out of the ordinary. However, she was wearing her long corduroy skirt, which fell nearly to her shins and which, now that she was lying down, was stretched taut across her thighs. They both recoiled at Teddy's maneuver, which on his end felt a little like doing a knee drop on a trampoline. With a little smile Cindy pulled herself away from him and sat on her legs at the head of the bed where she swayed for a minute on her many pillows before she got her balance.

"I just moved here," she said.

"Well, last summer," Teddy said.

"And sometimes I forget we don't know each other very well."

Teddy pulled himself into a semi-reclining position, something like the one the nude woman assumed in the painting in the cartoon. Deciding instantaneously that this attitude was either too seductive or too fetal for the circumstances, whatever they now were, he sat the rest of the way up and leaned back against the wall. "I thought we were getting along very well, not just tonight, but also tonight."

"We were," Cindy said. "We are. We're talking."

She seemed unsure whether to pick at her skirt or at the bedspread.

"There's something I've been wanting to say, but never found the right time. And that's sort of relevant."

"All right," Teddy said.

"Teddy, you know I like you."

She reached over and pulled on his hand. His arm flapped like a rope dangling from his shoulder.

"But sometimes I get the feeling that you expect things to happen on a certain schedule, one that you've decided on long in advance, by yourself, in private, like just now."

"That's where you're wrong," Teddy said.

"Oh?" Cindy asked. "How?"

"I'm way ahead of schedule."

"What do you mean?"

"I've seen you naked."

"You've what?" Cindy said with a startled laugh. "When?"

"I guess I never told you," Teddy said. "It was at the Chapel Gate meet."

Briefly he imagined himself hanging from that humid wood in the midst of leaves, while at the moment the brick walls of Cindy's house radiated cold all around them.

"I climbed up the locker room wall and looked in the window. . . fanlight. . . whatever it is."

"Oh," Cindy said. "That was you?"

"It wasn't my idea. I did it for the team. I guess they assumed Chapel Gate's girls would be in there. It was for revenge. No, I did it for Billy. They were going to make him do it, because he blew the meet. You remember? The false start?"

"Well," Cindy said. "How did I look?"

"If I told you how beautiful you were, you wouldn't believe

me."

"And were you going to undress me now?"

"I don't know," Teddy said. "I don't think so."

"I don't think so, either," Cindy said. "I think you just felt it was time to do something else. I'm not really even talking about the physical stuff. You have been unusually polite, believe me. It's more general. It's that you seem to want things to be a certain way. Do you remember the time I came to see you at work?"

"Yes," Teddy said.

"I could tell the minute I got there I shouldn't have come. I understood then that you wanted to see me, or me to see you, but only in certain situations. You wanted me to see you as a swimmer, or as a student, but not as a kid cutting grass. I think friends should be happy to see each other anytime," she said and paused. "It was the same at the second Chapel Gate meet. Do you remember that day?"

"Yes," Teddy said again.

He remembered all too well. He remembered the girl in the filter room. He hadn't exactly thrown her phone number away. He had put the slip of paper in the center drawer of his desk, where he could trust it soon to be indistinguishable from the many empty gum wrappers it contained. He thought he had seen the girl once since then, pushing a shopping cart for her mother, or at any rate an older woman, in the grocery store. He had cut down another aisle. And he remembered the relay where his brothers switched places before his very eyes.

"I knew what you were doing. You could have swum that day, your shoulder was well enough; but you wanted to give Hooty a chance to swim. That was nice of you, but it was all inside your head. Everything had to come out right. You would rather see your friends win than win yourself. I don't think anyone guessed it, but me. You didn't pay much attention to me that day, and that's because you don't like to think of me as a swimmer. I'm your girlfriend. You're the swimmer. Your brother Chip did. He took me seriously as a swimmer. That's all he thought of me as, but that's another story."

"Do you want to break up?" Teddy asked.

"Were you listening to me?" Cindy retorted.

"I was sitting right here the whole time."

Cindy sighed and said, "Maybe we shouldn't see each other for a little while."

Teddy sat still for a minute or two.

"Would you do me a favor? For old times' sake?"he asked.

"Teddy," Cindy said, shoving against his shoulder. "I didn't say I never wanted to see you again."

"Would you go out with my brother?"

Cindy sat back against her headboard.

"Which one?" she asked.

Outside, looking up as he got in his car, wherever he looked in the sky, Teddy still could see only one star at a time. It was probably a little colder, but it seemed no nearer to Christmas than it had four hours before this.

CHAPTER SEVENTEEN

Out of Order

"How did this happen?" Chip Livingstone was asking. "Who's responsible?"

As of a few hours before on this Saturday evening in December of 1967, the Christmas meet was over, although the holiday, itself, was still to come. The couch that Chip had slept on, if intermittently, during the visit of his girlfriend Susan, and on which he currently sat, had been pushed aside from the picture window in the living room to make way for the Christmas tree, decorated, except for the tinsel, which according to Livingstone family tradition was not added until Christmas Eve. The few presents scattered around the base of the tree were from more or less distant relatives. Gifts within the immediate family were also not put out until the night before Christmas and were opened only in the morning.

"No one blames you. That's the main thing," Mr. Livingstone said. "It's just a rule."

"I was ready," Chip said, looking in Teddy's direction as he uncharacteristically repeated himself. "I was ready."

Billy Livingstone, the middle brother of three, was not present. He was attending the post-meet party. The three other males in the family sat in the living room while Mrs. Livingstone prepared their supper in the kitchen. The heavy and not especially seasonal aroma of spaghetti sauce clung to the walls of the room like a coat of paint. Mr. Livingstone and sons looked as though they were awaiting the outcome of an emergency operation rather than dinner. Teddy would not have been surprised to look down and find a circular table full of the latest issues of Modern Surgery magazine in front of him.

When Chip suddenly slammed his fist into his open hand, Teddy reflected that anger was his brother's least frequent as well as his least attractive mood.

"Why did this have to happen?" Chip said, then simplified his question. "What happened?"

Well, Chip, a lot happened.

My brother Billy was not the only resident of our neighborhood who had recently gotten serious about swimming.

One night, a week or so before the big meet, I went down to Hooty's house. On our way from the front hall to his bedroom we passed the open door of his father's study. The walls were solid books. You had to wedge your hand between two shelves to locate the light switch. Very few of the volumes had jackets, and their bindings were often frayed like old carpet. Some shelves were packed with magazines that Mr. Hurwitz called journals. Elbow deep in papers, he sat at the long work table that took up the middle of the room. He was in his usual lounging attire, suit pants and an open white dress shirt. I considered him balder than my father, not so much in surface area as in effect. He combed his remaining hair back along the sides of his head like wings on a helmet. With his glasses pushed up as he stared down at his desk, the top of his head was a face in itself. Then he looked up at us.

"What have you gotten me into here, Howard?" he asked.

"Me?" Hooty questioned, deceptively innocently.

Each leaning on his own jamb, we stopped in the doorway.

"Who am I, the Postmaster General?" Mr. Hurwitz asked.

The mounds of paper that he gestured at I knew to be entry forms for the Christmas meet. Perhaps as some kind of parental penance, Mr. Hurwitz had volunteered to be meet coordinator. I had never so much as seen him in the stands at a little league meet before this. Every year a different adult assumed this duty. My mother had done it the first year Chip swam for Norm, turning our family room into an archives. At one end of Mr. Hurwitz's desk sat a rule book like the one Chip had lent me, but in mint condition. Apparently, the cover had originally been red and blue. Hooty's father got up from his chair, but was prevented from truly pacing by the fact that he was wearing bedroom slippers. It was more of a shuffle.

"Look at me," he said. "I am modern man in his self-created environment of pressure, nothing but pressure, unrelenting pressure resulting in anxiety. What possessed me to get involved in this?"

All at once I could account for the preternaturally blank expression Hooty could produce at will. It was the perfect complement to his father's animation!

"I thought this was supposed to be good fun," Mr. Hurwitz went on in the absence of an explanation from his son. "You can't believe what deadly earnest people are in about all this. Forms keep coming in and mothers call. Some kids are entered in eight events. There are six year old girls swimming!"

"Relax, Dad," Hooty said, although transparently trying to work him further into his frenzy. "There's still a week to go."

"That's right," Mr. Hurwitz said, glaring in agreement.

“Five more days for forms to come in to me! The deadline was supposedly yesterday, but what are we going to do, send them back to Virginia in their bathing suits?” He asked rhetorically as he wheeled back to his table, picked up an envelope and brandished it. “This one’s postmarked Virginia!”

Hooty examined the envelope.

“Northern Virginia. It’s from a suburb of Washington, DC, probably.”

“Thank you, Rand McNally,” Mr. Hurwitz said, snatching the envelope back.

“Look, Dad; it’s really a very simple process,” Hooty said. “It’s just a matter of putting all the forms in order. First you group them by event, for instance girls’ eleven and twelve fifty-yard backstroke. Then you arrange those forms from slowest to fastest and divide them into stacks of eight. Each stack is a heat. See?”

“I’m so ashamed of myself that I don’t more often stop to be grateful that I raised a child prodigy,” Mr. Hurwitz said. “Now would you like to do my taxes for me?” he asked as suddenly, comically, his expression clouded over. “Hey, get out of here,” he said. “You’re not supposed to see any of this. This is top secret stuff!” he shouted as he waved us out of the doorway and down the hall toward Hooty’s room. “I’m calling the AAU, the FBI and the CIA,” he called after us. “Right now. I’ve got them on the line.”

Mr. Hurwitz was at his most amusing when annoyed. Whereas with most adults, it was vice versa.

Chip looked up at his father and shook his head. "Do you think somebody could have done it on purpose?" he asked.

He wore a very puzzled frown, as though, after all, the strangeness of the case precluded anger, outrage, or any of the more elemental emotions, and Mr. Livingstone shrugged.

"I forget, what are you swimming in the Christmas meet?"

Hooty and I had settled onto the floor of his bedroom. I sat cross-legged on an oriental rug, which in turn lay on the blue wall-to-wall carpet. As a kid I had often pretended to myself that this same rectangle of rug was a raft that I had to steer over an expanse of ocean, and I would have been embarrassed to admit that that mental image persisted into my waning adolescence. Hooty had put on his sunglasses and set his electric keyboard across his lap. The possibility that at any minute he might reach for his headphones lent to this, as to all my questions, a certain urgency.

"The hundred free," he said. "That's all I qualified to swim, barely."

"There are always the relays," I said.

This consolation was not as hollow as Hooty's smirk

implied. Once a club had qualified a relay for the meet, it could put any members of the team it wanted to on the relay. Lineups were often juggled as the meet unfolded. I had already witnessed this practice at various times, and had since found it sanctioned in black and white in the rule book Chip gave me. Furthermore, even our tentative lineups weren't set. Norm would enter several relays, both freestyle and medley; and he would decide their composition on the basis of time trials to be held the following day. Of course, every older boy wanted to be on one or both of the A relay teams. I knew that the one smirk was meant to cover all these contingencies.

"Somebody could get sick," I continued. "One of the swimmers on our team could turn out to be a Nazi war criminal and be disqualified, a very young one. You could beat somebody in the time trial tomorrow."

Subtly, but clearly in response to the last of these three scenarios, Hooty said, "Don't be ridiculous."

"People could think I did it," Chip said as he directed this remark to his brother Teddy, for the sake perhaps of even-handedness or just variety. "I mean, they naturally would assume I did it. I'm the obvious one."

"It was a simple mistake," Mr. Livingstone said.

"Well," Chip asked, "who made it?"

The atmosphere before the time trials at practice the next day was not so much strained as just strange. For the past couple of weeks we had been doing "quality" rather than "quantity" workouts. In other words, we had been swimming shorter but harder sets, trying to develop speed now that we had presumably acquired some endurance by dint of our innumerable laps earlier in the season. Quantity and quality workouts had in common that they were numbingly painful. Just recently, however, we had entered the period immediately preceding a big meet known as "tapering." I had heard of this process from Chip and his friends and instinctively dreaded it, but what it amounted to was doing nothing. That was worse.

True, this was a minor taper, since we were really at the outset of the winter season. Twice a year, in early spring and again at the end of the summer, swimmers tapered in earnest, shaving their bodies and inducing a two-day pre-meet coma in order to conserve every erg their cells could produce for the upcoming race, but some guys couldn't handle even the present reprieve. You could watch their nerves snap before your very eyes. They would drag themselves as usual from the locker room onto the pool deck, feigning the foreboding that would precede a full workout. They would lead everyone to believe they were getting into the water just to loosen up, only to break greedily into a set of sprints. Those swimmers who kept their composure couldn't warm up too languidly to suit Norm. Once he even yelled at guys for working too hard.

Moreover, in the course of the past week we new swimmers had made a sobering discovery about our coach. He did have a sense of humor. The booming laughs of the early season proved as perfunctory as they sounded. What Norm turned out to really find amusing was staging a mock meet during practice where we all swam unfamiliar and/or fictitious events. I had had to race Fichter in a fifty-yard individual medley, switching strokes halfway down each length. Leo beat me at that, too. Norm chortled.

Our only exertion during this period took the form of time trials, and by the time they arrived they were welcome. Maybe that was the point. Over the last couple of days before the meet we would all swim each of our events all-out, both to simulate competition and to decide who would swim the various relays. The previous day had been devoted to strokes. Today would be a cavalcade of freestyle events. As one heat after another was performed under Norm's vigilant stopwatch, the rest of us sat around seeing who could look the most torpid, which got to be an effort in itself. Hooty swam in the penultimate heat of the hundred. Slumped against the clammy tile wall next to the water fountain, I watched him thresh his way through four lengths of freestyle. He still had that sidewinding stroke, recovering his left arm like a sickle every time he breathed. It was plain to see he had been attending no coaching clinics lately. Still, he turned in a good time, but not a great time.

The last heat of the day bore a striking resemblance to the lineup for the infamous descending fifties of a few weeks previous to this. Since his dressing down by Norm, Chip had spouted his times on demand like an accountant. He was also more inclined of late to cite unsolicited facts, and he seemed generally more worried, both probably because he was in the middle of final exams. He had taken one earlier that very day. He climbed onto the block in lane four. Between him and me, Leo Fichter seemed untroubled by tests or anything else. I couldn't tell how Billy was comporting himself on the other side of Chip. All I could be reasonably certain of was that all eight of us in the heat would be shaking out our feet and hands in the standard pre-race ritual, like some kind of topless all male chorus line, until Norm called us to our marks. At the gun—another realistic detail—we all launched ourselves into the void of a watery minute, more or less. At the other end, the results were as expected, or at least not unexpected. Chip had touched out Fichter, and a couple of seconds later I had touched out Billy. As the top four finishers, we were ipso facto the A four by one hundred-yard freestyle relay team.

"Almost an all-Livingstone relay," Norm mused as he cleared his watch. "Listen, would your father be free on Saturday?"

"What?" Billy asked, hauling himself dripping onto the deck and making a sweeping gesture back down toward Fichter who was still hanging on the lane marker. "Haven't I introduced you to our long lost brother Leo?"

"Leo Livingstone," Norm said. "It has a nice ring to it."

"I'd take it over Fichter," Leo said, back on dry land now himself. "It doesn't get you into as much trouble if you mispronounce it."

There it was, perhaps the most ominous note of the day. Leo Fichter had produced a witticism, and at his own expense.

"Don't get me wrong," Mr. Livingstone said. "Howie Hurwitz is a bright guy, but not too practical, if you know what I mean."

Had he been called on to explicate his father's remark, Teddy would have said that he meant, and was correct in saying, that alone among the garages of the neighborhood that of the Hurwitzes contained no power saw.

"It's just that he could easily get things mixed up. And what possible motive would you have for doing that?"

Chip looked at Teddy again.

The Thursday before the meet was also the last day of school before Christmas. When Christmas and New Year's Day fell on a Monday, as they did this year, you stood to get badly stiffed on your school vacation, whereas if they fell in the middle of a week you might get a couple of extra days thrown in on either end. This year we got a break in that we at least got the Friday preceding Christmas off from school. Chip was coming home tomorrow, and all his exams were over; but he made it clear that his grades would not arrive until after the holidays.

As so often lately, I walked into our bedroom that night to find Billy at his desk. In my festive mood I spared his homework the show of disgust it deserved on the eve of a vacation. At second glance, I could see my brother did not have an open book in front of him. Neither was a writing utensil to be seen on the surface of the desk. Rather, Billy sat before a single sheet of paper. The envelope that had presumably contained it had on its upper left-hand corner not only a printed return address but a seal of some kind. Then I re-revised my initial impression. Billy wasn't reading the document, he was staring at it. Anyway, it couldn't have taken that long to read two short paragraphs.

"What are you doing?" I asked softly, as always not overhasty in assessing my brother's current level of consciousness.

"It's a letter from a college," Billy said. "I got in."

He handed me the letter and, as an afterthought, the envelope along with it. I knew the name of the school and even, on closer inspection, recognized the seal. I had seen it on the sweatshirt a friend of mine had come back from a summer vacation in New England wearing.

"Already?" I asked, even though I had the announcement in my hand in writing, along with the very explicit promise of further communication to follow it.

"Early admission," Billy said.

"Are you going?"

"I have to, pretty much. That's the deal on early admission."

Holding on to the letter, I sank slowly behind Billy to sit on the edge of his bed. Anyone who walked through the door at that juncture would have thought the letter was addressed to me. Silence reigned in the room until I thought of something to say.

"Will you swim there?"

"I don't know if I'll keep that up," Billy said.

He had swiveled in his chair to face me. Our knees nearly touched.

"I'm not even sure they have a team."

I could have told them they did. After a brief review of my

mental files, I had recovered not only the name and location of the college in question but also the salient points of its promotional literature. Billy had routinely passed along to me all the college catalogues he got in the mail after he read them. They joined Chip's rule book in the growing stack of documents between my bed and the wall. I could have reminded him that the student body of this private four-year liberal arts college was encouraged to balance academics, athletics and social life in the pursuit of a diverse educational experience, how (to judge from the photographic evidence) students of both sexes spent their mornings circling bearded professors on the grassy knolls of the campus and adjourned to the pool, practice room or snack bar in the afternoon. In all three which places they apparently continued to discuss the same burning issues. I could have told him the average SAT scores of entering freshmen. But that matter was now academic in every sense of the word. Billy had obviously comfortably exceeded the minimum requirements for admission to the school. So we sat a little while longer in silence.

"I hope this last year hasn't been too bad for you," Billy said at last, not particularly to the point.

From his first words alone, however, or maybe just from the tone of his voice, I could tell that what would follow would be self-contained, without context and also unavoidable.

"So far, I mean, since Chip left. I know I haven't acted like that much of an older brother. Oldest brother, now. I can't remember taking you aside and giving you any advice, but that was on purpose. Even if I had any advice to give, I decided a long time ago that I would always, and especially if I was ever in this position, be exactly the opposite kind of brother to you that Chip was to me, in *every* respect.

"The problem is that one of those respects is that he's likable. That's another thing I decided years ago. Certain people are just naturally likable, like being tall, or blonde, or musical. Chip is likable. He's not always that nice, but he's still likable. People like him. I like him. Even when he beat me up as a kid I think we both understood that as a sign of affection, or connection. He didn't enjoy keeping me in line. He took it upon himself as a duty. It was as though he was sparing Dad a chore, like cutting the grass without being asked. Come to think of it, Chip didn't cut the grass that much. Maybe he beat me up instead. I read once in a magazine—it was pretty straightforward for the most part, you know, naked women—but in one part it said that inflicting pain could be an expression of love. Maybe Chip belongs to that school of thought," he paused. "The problem is, how do you be the opposite of someone likable? Well, that's not a problem. That's simple." He stopped again, then said, "Does that make any sense?"

"There is one thing about which I'm still not clear," I said.

"What?" Billy asked.

"Do you still have that magazine?"

Billy gave me a look.

"Well," I said, "you obviously won't be giving me any more college catalogues to read."

"What? You mean some kind of prank, practical joke?" Mr. Livingstone asked, not perhaps following Chip's train of thought quite so closely as Teddy was.

"I don't think that would be the word for it," Chip said.

"Then I still don't see the motive," Mr. Livingstone said. "Sorry."

"Well, who would benefit?" Chip asked. "You hear about coaches doing this, to qualify swimmers or improve their chances to place."

"Not Norm Cohen," Mr. Livingstone said. "He wouldn't risk his reputation like that. And anyway, the whole point was to see what you and Fichter would do head-to-head."

"Correct," Chip said. "We can eliminate Norm."

"Another swimmer?" Mr. Livingstone said. "Fichter?"

This possibility Chip rejected with a shake of his head. "Fichter wouldn't really have cared what happened in the two hundred. He'll swim some event or other for Norm during the season, one of the sprints, or the IM. No, I mean someone who would benefit purely from my misfortune. I'm thinking closer to home, although not at the moment."

CHAPTER EIGHTEEN

The Return of Montefeltro

"I've always wondered about that," Teddy said. "But it just now occurred to me. Does that make any sense?"

"Not a great deal," Reverend Burns said. "But I know what you mean. Isn't it funny how that works? You realize that you know something."

"Or, maybe I realized that I had been thinking something over for as long as I could remember, because I'm still not sure I know anything."

"Run it by me again."

"A lot of things in the Bible happen in threes, like the three wise men, three days in the belly of the whale, or in the parable of the talents—the three servants."

"Sure," Reverend Burns said. "It's like in a joke. You have to set up the punch line. First comes the priest, then the Levite, then—bang—the Good Samaritan! Get it?"

"But in all the stories I can think of in the Bible about brothers, there are just two, starting with Cain and Abel, then Ishmael and Isaac."

"Jacob and Esau! You're on to something," Reverend Burns said. "And, if you notice, God seems to favor the younger brother. He always seems to be the clever one. That's being too polite. He's the sneaky one. Sometimes there are a lot of brothers, like Joseph's David had seven."

"But brothers don't come in threes."

"Not that I can think of right off hand."

"The disciples come in pairs. There are James and John, Peter and Andrew."

"Well, Jesus and James," Reverend Burns said.

"So what use is a third brother?" Teddy asked. "I can think of times when one would have come in handy, especially in one story Jesus tells about brothers that has always bothered me."

"Let's see if I can guess," Reverend Burns said, "the parable of the Prodigal Brother! I mean, the Prodigal Son."

"For one thing," Teddy said, "no matter what parable it is, I always end up cheering for the wrong guy."

"For example?" Reverend Burns asked.

"All right. Wouldn't you think the master would come home from his trip and praise the guy who buried his talent? Wouldn't that be like the pearl of great price? Why doesn't the master say, 'You good and faithful servant! You valued the talent I gave you so highly you didn't risk it for a 500% or even a 1000% return like these two reckless, materialistic bums. Take all the money they earned for yourself. I'm going to kick them into the outer darkness. For he who hangs on to even the little that he has, it turns out, will end up with more than he ever dreamed of having.' But I'm on the wrong side, as usual."

"That's the point of the parables, it seems to me," Reverend Burns said. "Think of him as Jesus, the stand-up rabbi. And the joke's on you. Jesus said you're not supposed to understand his stories. You're supposed to resist understanding, then surrender and just believe they make sense. Why? Well, maybe then you'll have faith in your own life. Your life is a story. It makes sense, whether or not it ends happily. Jesus' didn't. Your life has a plot. And you're the hero."

"And is the parable really about talents?" Teddy asked. "Did I get one?"

"A talent is a Greek measure of weight. It's just a coincidence that 'talent' means something else in English. I guess

I've always thought that everyone's identity counts as a talent. The one thing you can do that no one else can. On the other hand, being yourself is not difficult—in fact, you can't help but do it—so I don't know that you'd consider it an ability."

"But back to the Prodigal Son," Teddy said. "It's hard for me to read, because I'm not in it. I'm watching it from the outside."

"You know, I believe there is a missing son in that picture. I didn't know it was you. I once preached a sermon. 'The Third Brother,' I think I called it. It was not my most inspired title. Of course you remember the sermon I preached a couple of years ago on those other brothers you mentioned in Genesis 4, 'Will God Be Abel to Raise Cain?'"

I can quote all your sermons by heart," Teddy said.

"You wouldn't lie to your pastor, would you?"

"Not on a Sunday."

"This is Friday."

"I wondered why no one else was here."

On the Friday of the last full week of classes before Christmas vacation, Teddy had taken the long way home from school. In fact, he had gone the opposite way, up over the hill toward Fox Chapel Road, joining some walkers who lived in that direction. He had just spent the day in class with most of them, but in these unaccustomed circumstances they greeted him like an old acquaintance. They dropped their snowballs for small talk. It was like a high school reunion after ten minutes instead of ten years. He half-expected to be invited into someone's house for a cocktail, but he left them at Fox Chapel Presbyterian Church.

Inside, out of the glare of the clear winter day, the halls seemed dim before they seemed bright. The gym looked like a gym again. The double doors were locked, but each had a window into which he could peer. He had to put a hand over his eyes to see through his own reflection to a gray expanse of linoleum. You could no more imagine a dance taking place on that barren surface than you could imagine crops sprouting.

Reverend Burns' office was airy and bright, all modern furniture with metal tubing and a white carpet. It was so sunny outside you weren't sure if the lights were on or not. After a minute it seemed almost warm and breezy. Anyway, it was very comfortable. The blue sky through the windows could have been glazed with ice, but the piled-up snow was ebbing away from the edges of the parking lot, and the asphalt was drying up in patches.

"I wasn't sure you'd be here," Teddy said. "I thought maybe Friday and Saturday were a pastor's weekend. Obviously, you work on Sunday."

"On paper, Monday is my day off," Reverend Burns said. "I've tried Friday, but it doesn't work. There are too many odds

and ends that come up before the service. Once in a while you get a quiet Monday. But back to the Prodigal Son, again. I agree that you need another brother in that story. Those two are both in the wrong, wouldn't you say, each in his own way? Or, actually, they're wrong in the same way. They're both worried about the inheritance. They're both looking out for themselves. I know what I'm trying to say. Neither one can see outside himself. I hope I said that in my sermon. And that's where you come into the story. How did you put it? You felt as though you were watching from the outside? How would things have come out differently if there had been a third brother?"

"Or with Cain and Abel," Teddy said. "At least in the Prodigal Son story no one gets killed. And, as long as we're talking about Cain and Abel—and we are talking about them, aren't we?"

"That's what it sounds like," Reverend Burns said.

"What was so unacceptable about Cain's sacrifice, anyway?"

"There you have one of the great mysteries," Reverend Burns said. "No explanation offered, to us or to Cain, four chapters into the Bible. . . and I'm already confused."

"If you ask me, those weren't the real sacrifices—the meat and the grain."

"What, then?" Reverend Burns asked.

"The two of them together offered a human sacrifice. They were actually cooperating, not feuding. One of my brother's many theories is that, if he just hadn't done the first wrong thing he ever did, he wouldn't have done any of the other wrong things he went on to do. Or at least might not have. I'm not sure he realizes the pressure that would create. Maybe it's a blessing we can't be perfect. Maybe Cain and Abel sacrificed themselves for all future brothers. They set a nice, low standard. As long as you don't kill your brother you're an improvement. Cain and Abel had to act out the way brothers really feel about each other. That was their job. Abel sacrificed himself, maybe not knowingly; but he did. He couldn't be righteous forever. It wouldn't be fair. He died. Cain couldn't either. He sinned so that Abel wouldn't have to sin. But it could just have easily been the other way around, right? Even in the Old Testament God is like the master in the parable of the talents. He could have praised Cain for working the fields. Even though he survived, Cain may have made the greater sacrifice. He went around the rest of his life a marked man, didn't he?"

"He did."

"So he sacrificed forgiveness, too?"

"Remember, the mark protected him. Maybe it was a mark of forgiveness. I know you believe in forgiveness. Do you remember the theory you shared with me over the summer that you got from

reading Dante in school? About the character Montefeltro who got in trouble because he asked forgiveness in advance of the sin?"

"I remember. It was just a neat idea. I didn't really think it would work. But looking back I don't think that was my problem. It was just that I wasn't in my brothers' story. I was in no position to forgive or be forgiven. I couldn't forgive one brother, because I wasn't the one he had hurt. I couldn't ask forgiveness, because I hadn't hurt either one."

"It sounds as though you love both your brothers equally," Reverend Burns said. "You don't need to be forgiven for that."

"I'm willing to be forgiven," Teddy said. "At least now I know the order. First I have to commit a sin."

CHAPTER NINETEEN

Relay Order

The night before the meet I let myself into the Hurwitz's house by the side door. Whether or not school was in session, whenever our social schedules permitted, and they usually did, Hooty and I kicked off the weekend by watching a certain couple of television shows in his family room. On this Friday night Hooty and his parents were attending his sister's piano recital. Naturally, it was the Christmas recital, even though the Hurwitz family did not celebrate Christmas, but rather some other holiday about the same time of year. Every member of the Hurwitz family seemed to agree that Rachel was the more musically talented of the two children, although how you could tell this about an eleven year-old girl, I didn't know. My own contribution to the evening was to make sure that the TV was turned to the proper channel and warmed up so that Hooty could join the evening's programming in progress. The only objection to this arrangement came from my mother, who was horrified to learn that I planned to enter a vacant home and would apparently consent only if I could produce both an engraved invitation and a court-ordered search warrant.

The Hurwitzes on the other hand seemed to have as small a regard for security as they did for etiquette. A glance around the living room indeed revealed little that would or could be stolen. Every object in it seemed massive, wooden, rooted. For that matter, it was always hard for me to imagine how this arid living room could support life beyond the length of my own visits. The air was full of spices that did not in the slightest suggest food. But then, every one of my friend's homes was uniquely alien. In some, where onions seemed perpetually to be simmering, it was at least as difficult for me to breathe as it would have been in the plumed, purple atmosphere of the planet Jupiter as represented in my science books.

When I stepped out onto the hardwood floor of the living room, I felt as though I were the one on the stage of a concert hall, with the books on the shelves and the wooden masks on the walls as spectators. I suddenly wished I had prepared a few arias in case an accompanist should step out from behind the picture window curtains and pull the bench up to the grand piano. I guess it was a baby grand. In any case, the top could be opened and propped up.

In a minute my expectant audience dissolved back into the empty spaces of a split-level suburban home. I crossed the living room, climbed the three steps to the hallway and headed back to the family room. It was a good half hour until our first show started. I had no idea what would be on now.

"Oh, come on, now," Mr. Livingstone said. "You don't suspect your brother."

As Mrs. Livingstone entered the room, ostentatiously unaware of the tenor of the conversation in progress, she skimmed Chip's hair. Very likely she had envisaged a more substantial caress. But Chip, alerted perhaps by a few early micro volts of static electricity, ducked his head. Then he ran his own hand across his hair.

"What happened today was unfortunate, but it's not really what's bothering Chip," Mrs. Livingstone said, demonstrating once again her gift for the third person.

Chip held his mother's gaze until his will to incomprehension gave out.

"It's no tragedy, Mom," he said, to judge by his tone, not for the first time.

Mrs. Livingstone sat down straight-backed on the edge of a chair, at ease but on duty.

"Well, but you don't have a date for the party."

"I wouldn't have gone anyway," Chip said, "not under the circumstances."

"When Billy gets home we can eat," Mrs. Livingstone said.

"Then we can get some answers," Chip said.

For as many years as I had been keeping mental records, the weather right before Christmas in my native Pittsburgh had been inappropriately mild. On the day of Christmas Eve you'd more likely play basketball in your driveway than ice skate on some pond. Later, wearing an overcoat to the candlelight service at church would be discretionary. Then January would arrive like an ice age. With or without snow, the air would go a frigid, flaky gray, and the ground would seem bleached with cold.

The day of the Christmas meet, Chip, Billy and I walked up the hill on the back side of Trees Hall in almost spring like warmth. There was a premature scent of mud in the air. We had a long hike, because all available parking spaces around the pool were taken. The buses that packed the curb out front represented various commercial lines, but they could have been painted in team colors—green and yellow, red and black. The abbreviation stenciled on their doors after the name of the city where the bus company was headquartered was most often the heartwarming "Pa.," but "W. Va."

and "Oh." were not uncommon.

Inside the building, it looked as though a campground had moved indoors. All along the upper hallway, from the front door onward, swimmers spread towels on top of the concrete as though it was grass. Some of them were playing cards. (At least no one had broken out a picnic lunch.) Farther down the hall, however, by the door to the courtyard, there was a makeshift concession booth, the aromas emanating from which advertised the same refreshments that would have been available at any high school football game—i. e., hot dogs, potato chips and the vinegary Coke mixed on the spot from those tanks that looked as though they could easily be converted to produce rocket fuel. A very few of the swimmers were sampling this fare between events. It was more for the parents and/or spectators. A silver-haired man in a plaid hunting jacket took his place in the line as we passed it on our way to the stairs. No one seated or standing in the hall so much as winced at the random gunfire from the pool where the heats for the eight and under swimmers must have been under way—unless they had an infant and/or toddler age group to get through first. The scene in the hall reminded me of accounts I had read in Civil War history books of families making an outing of watching the first battle of Bull Run.

For most of the year, and especially when Pitt was on vacation, we were used to having the dressing rooms downstairs pretty much to ourselves. Ordinarily, I liked to spread my clothes over several lockers, taking one half-sized floor-level unit for my shoes alone. Today, I would not have that luxury. Every last locker was crammed with clothes, towels, and sweats. Combination locks had blossomed on some of them. Half-naked strangers clustered conspiratorially in every aisle. The showers were full of guys still or already in their suits. Some stretched while others bowed their heads meditatively under the spray. The stalls in the bathroom were full at all times, with a more or less continuous flush creating the sound effect of a subterranean torrent. I watched one guy lean down and apparently spot a familiar pair of sweat pants ringing someone's ankles. With dawning suspicion, he said, "Are you in there again, Wordle?" It was true that for many swimmers a pre-race trip to the can was a matter more of ritual than necessity.

As soon as we were dressed in our suits or, as the case may have been, undressed to our suits (foreseeing the chaos in the locker room, I had worn my tank suit under my pants in lieu of underwear) we stepped through the shower room, dodging the steam-spouts on either side that encased the stretching swimmers. Among them, not surprisingly, was Fichter, who nodded to us as we went out onto the pool deck. The sudden space came as a relief. That bright cavern of a natatorium seemed able to absorb any din. A slight breeze circulated. We headed along the side of the main pool, in the deep end of which the races were taking place, to the next room and then to the practice pool. Of the three Livingstone boys, only Billy was swimming anything but the two hundred free, which was the last event of the day before the relays; but Chip (as we knew) believed in warming up early and often.

Almost immediately, we ran into Hooty, who hauled himself out of the seething warm-up lanes. He had driven down to the meet first thing in the morning with his father. Like Billy, he was swimming the hundred free, only a few events distant. After an exchange of pleasantries and prognostications among the four of us, I accompanied Hooty back the way I had just come to the officials' table, where we would all have to check in at some point before our respective heats. A race among maybe eleven and twelve year-old girls was just concluding. They all lifted their faces after they touched with that expression of solemn exhaustion characteristic of their age group. Up above the deep end the bleachers were reasonably full, fuller at least than I had ever seen them. This crowd was in constant motion. People came and went after each event. All the adults looked somewhat official to me. That is, it was hard to tell parents and coaches apart, if indeed there was any essential difference between them. At the officials' table we encountered a haggard but rather self-satisfied-looking Howard Hurwitz, Sr. His eyes were so ringed you might think they could be, and (in fact now needed to be) focused like the lenses on a pair of binoculars.

"I got it all straight at four o'clock this morning." He said, and his smile sagged before it was fully in place. "It's running like a top, a breeze."

Even as he spoke, however, a parent approached him from one side; and he reached instinctively for the rule book that lay on the table in front of him.

I started to walk away while Hooty confirmed his seeding, only to be stopped short by a sudden exclamation.

"Holy mother of Moses!"

"Watch your language, Hooty," I said over my shoulder. "We're in a swimming pool."

Then I turned to see him looking at the long strips of paper taped to the wall that listed all the day's upcoming events, heat by heat. I assumed Hooty was checking to see how his race was shaping up; but actually, he was looking much farther along.

"Chip is seeded number one in the two hundred," Hooty said as he pointed to lane four, heat four of the event. "I didn't know he was that fast. When did he do that time?"

"Some time trial during the fall, I guess," I said.

Satisfied, Hooty headed back toward the locker room to sequester himself in a toilet stall before his race. For my part, I walked all the way around to the far side of the pool, where I had the unforeseen pleasure of locating a bench, unoccupied and unclaimed by any swimming accessory, next to the sliding glass doors, which were open a crack onto the glassy cool air beyond. I lay down in my sweat suit on my back and turned my head open-eyed away from the gently sloping sunlight outside. The interior of the natatorium was not markedly more chaotic when rotated ninety degrees. I then closed my eyes for an indeterminate though never less than semi-conscious interval. When I opened them again, I saw a familiar figure approaching. To judge by its carriage, it was one of my brothers, swathed beyond immediate recognition in a sweat suit, one towel draped around its neck and another over his head. If I was not mistaken, this mountain of terry cloth was approaching Mohammed. It was Chip. Before I could stir to make space for him to sit down next to me, he stopped in front of me and spoke.

"I want you to know that for the past couple of weeks I've been thinking about what you told me," he began. "That night in my room? You were right. Today I'm taking your advice. I'm not looking ahead, behind or to either side. You may have noticed that I entered the two hundred today and no other individual event. That's because today I have one object, and that's to beat Fichter. Like you said, everything hinges on that. I might have placed better in the five hundred. Well, I won't even say that. I'm swimming the two hundred. I'll have plenty left over for the relay."

A smile glimmered in the shadow of the towel that hung over his brow.

"You can carry me through the relay, anyway. Thanks."

From flat on my back, I nodded in silent acknowledgment and watched Chip recede toward the practice pool. Regardless of any other revisions of his basic outlook, he would immerse himself a couple more times before the two hundred.

My training techniques in the water might not as yet have produced a world record, but I was perhaps unique among competitive swimmers in the art of simulating suspended animation immediately before any major race. After another bout of oblivion, the back of my skull finally rocking to a rest on the wooden bench, I roused myself to walk over to the practice pool, where I put in a few laps and several turns and declared myself warmed up for my race. Then I returned to the bench I had been monopolizing to find it sat on, lain under and leaned up against by several members of either sex and different ages of a rival club. In their identical sweat suits and various postures, they looked like a family trapeze act between shows.

The loss of the bench was of no great disappointment or inconvenience, because when I glanced up toward the bleachers, I saw that Cindy had arrived. At that distance, it was actually her sweater I recognized, green with rings of red and white. I suddenly realized it was seasonal, or that it was suddenly seasonal. I didn't bother waving to her. She might as well have been on the other side of the Grand Canyon. I just retraced the route through the locker room and up the fire stairs to the stands, which I entered several rows above Cindy's. Taking benches in my stride as though they were steps, I picked my way down to Cindy through several clumps of spectators and sat next to her.

We didn't say much. I thanked her for coming. She told me that her parents had dropped her off on their way to an afternoon social function. She was a little late. They would be a little early. Cindy wore her sweater over a corduroy skirt that I knew to actually be a jumper. Since under my sweatsuit, which I had unbuttoned almost to the waist, the viscosity of the liquid beading along my breastbone indicated perspiration to me rather than residual pool water, I was afraid Cindy must be very warm in her near-formal wear. I imagined her sweater acting as a kind of chlorine filter, swelling with the fumes the pool exhaled. But her skin stayed cool and clear.

Sitting silently high over this placid body of water next to a pretty, fully-clothed girl, I rediscovered how graceful swimming could be. I remembered why I had wanted to be part of the picture I was viewing once again. I had joined Cindy just before the last heat of the five hundred yard freestyle for the open male division—the only age group that swam that distance in the Christmas meet. It was an event that Chip would ordinarily have entered. There were plenty of other excellent swimmers on hand, college swimmers representing their home clubs, maybe treating the meet as one last time trial before their season began.

At the gun, these contestants all sprang off the blocks, punching eight crisp holes in the water as though it were a sheet of paper. In no hurry to start stroking with a long race ahead of them, they came up half a length later with kicks that produced a surprisingly delicate rustle from that far away from us. The first swimmer to breathe was frowning, as though in apology. Bunched together for the first few lengths, these guys turned almost in unison, eight pairs of feet slapping the wall as they flipped; then the silence of the push-off underwater until they surfaced and the pulse of their kicks resumed. Once the swimmers settled in, the occasional cheers of the fans sounded like afterthoughts. Their echoes ricocheted around the concrete rafters far overhead. This five hundred free went to form in that the outside lanes dropped off the pace first, and the race came down to a sprint between lanes four and five. With a last lunge, the swimmer in lane four won.

A couple of events later, we watched Fichter win the two hundred yard individual medley. He rocked his way effortlessly through the butterfly and the backstroke, but he clinched his victory with his strong, thrusting breast stroke, the pivotal leg of the race, since if you got a lead there, you could begin the freestyle, the final as well as the fastest stroke of the IM, while your opponents were still laboring through the breast stroke, losing ground. I found myself not only explaining this to Cindy but, in between, cheering for my bosom teammate Leo.

Not very hospitably, Norm Cohen's club always won its own meet, if only because we entered the most swimmers. Behind Fichter and our several child prodigies, we were right on schedule for another triumph. On the deck below Cindy and me, one heat, one event smoothly replaced another, with only an occasional conference at the officials' table to interrupt the flow. Dressed slightly more elegantly than usual for the occasion in a short-sleeved, button-down shirt instead of a tee shirt over his shorts, Norm made a little ceremony of walking each of his swimmers down to the blocks for the start of a race. At his seat at the officials' table, Mr. Hurwitz's wide and also dark-eyed expression suggested that on his emotional spectrum that particular day, alertness shaded directly into panic.

In the upcoming event his son, Howard Hurwitz, Jr., and my brother, Billy, took their marks for the hundred free. They had been seeded in the same heat, the next to fastest one—Billy toward the center and a less than ordinarily stone-faced Hooty in the outside lane closest to us. This race demonstrated once again that Billy had become the better swimmer. He won the heat by a body length over his closest rival, by two over Hooty. Even so, he would not place overall. The fast heat proved to be quite fast.

The couple of events that followed were of less personal interest to Cindy and me, but we sat and watched. Some of the girls turned in impressive times. With a shudder, Cindy recognized a couple of the bruisers from the summer league. In the silence that followed one clamorously close finish, Cindy looked down at the mimeographed sheet that served as a program for the meet. "Didn't you say you were swimming the two hundred freestyle?" she asked. When I said yes she then asked, "Isn't that the next event?"

I was standing on the pool deck when the gun sounded for the first heat of the two hundred free. Once I had arrived, slightly winded from my sprint down the fire stairs, I decided I would have enough to time to jump in the practice pool, as much to cool off as anything else. My qualifying time had earned me an outside lane in the event's final heat, still some ten minutes in the future. When I re-entered the natatorium, however, toweling off after my last-minute warm-up, it was not to join a stately, Olympic-like procession of swimmers to the starting blocks. Rather, you would have thought a food riot had broken out in a Calcutta market, given the half-naked youths and flustered looking men in shorts who swarmed around the officials' table.

"What does that do to the lane assignments?" one of my co-contestants asked another, not too alarmed not to pull one heel up behind him to the small of his back, yoga-like.

I tried without success to learn from Chip what was amiss. He brushed by me with no sign of recognition, his face blurred with emotion, seemingly on the point of either rage or tears or both. It was Norm he was making for, all the while motioning back toward the table where Mr. Hurwitz was in animated discussion with a slender man with hair and beard, exactly the same shade of gray, like a pelt, whom I recognized as the coach of another Pittsburgh swimming club.

As Chip accompanied Norm back along the side of the pool, I overheard him say, "It's an obvious mistake. I never swam anything close to that. That would be a meet record, wouldn't it? A state record? I don't know."

From behind the officials' table, the other coach addressed the advancing Norm Cohen.

"This boy's time called attention to itself," he said.

Despite his professorial air, the build beneath his golf shirt and shorts was lithe and athletic. I could see him dropping with that water-proof beard into the pool for a set with swimmers.

"My swimmer was somewhat taken aback to see he wasn't seeded higher. So was I."

"It's a mistake," Chip said. "I entered one fifty-five point zero. Not one fifty point five."

Throughout this exchange, Mr. Hurwitz had the rule book in his hands, flipping futilely from the table of contents toward the back.

"I'm sorry, Chip," he said, "but I think he's right. It's in here someplace about qualifying times, about accurate qualifying times."

With everyone by now standing around and waiting, Mr. Hurwitz continued to riffle frantically through the book. You hoped somebody would say something.

"Look in the appendix."

"Thank you, Teddy," Mr. Hurwitz said, turning straight to the back of the book. "Here it is, under 'Rules of Competition': 'a swimmer who either knowingly or unknowingly enters a false time for a qualifying time in a competition is subject to disqualification from that competition.'"

"So I'm out of the two hundred?" Chip asked.

"The competition, it says," the silver-haired coach said. "That means the meet."

As Chip spun away from the table, quivering with frustration on top of whatever now not-to-be-vented pre-race psych he had worked up, I followed him. From the bench where he had set all his stuff, and the edges of which he now gripped with both hands, bent over, I looked back to watch the continuing discussion. Norm argued for another minute or so with his colleagues. Then all at once he pulled his expression blank and taut as you would a sheet on a bed and walked away.

When he reached us he asked Chip, although without apparent anger, "Didn't you check the seedings?"

"No," Chip said.

"Let me guess," Norm said. "You didn't want to know about the competition beforehand."

"I already knew. Fichter was my competition," Chip said. "Then this happened. How?"

"We'll worry about that later," Norm said. "For now, we have to worry about making up your points."

With Norm between us, Fichter and I walked back toward the blocks, where order had finally been restored. While the timers took their places in each lane, some of the swimmers kneeled on the lip of the pool to scoop water over their shoulders. Norm turned to me and said, "If you do an impersonation of your brother, do it now."

So the final heat of the two hundred yard freestyle in the

open male division went off slightly behind schedule, and also with an empty lane in the middle, like a comb with a missing tine. The winner, representing the Erie Y, climbed out of the pool and into his YALE SWIMMING sweat suit. Chip would not have beaten him. Whether he would have beaten Fichter, who finished third in this slightly depleted field, would remain a mystery. I came in where I was supposed to come in, last—although with Chip out of the race, this was seventh rather than eighth place. On the other hand, I swam that distance faster than I ever had.

I really didn't have time to go up and see Cindy after my race. A scant few heats of breaststroke would intervene before the grand finale of the Christmas meet, the freestyle relays. Immediately after the two hundred free I lay down on a bench. Then I floated face-down in the practice pool, corpse-style. Then I lay down on the bench again. Five minutes before our race, Norm waved Fichter, Billy and me to the deep end where we huddled together under a cloudburst of cheering from the crowd as the older girls took the blocks for their relay. The problem was that, after Chip's disqualification, we were a three-man squad.

"We need a swimmer," Norm said matter-of-factly to his truncated relay team.

"Well, we came to the right place," Billy said.

"Seriously," Fichter said.

“I nominate Hooty Hurwitz,” I said.

“Come on,” Fichter spat as much as said, although he failed to complete his thought. “Come on. Get Jackson.”

“Jackson’s gone,” Billy said. “The party’s at his house. He and his parents left after the hundred.”

“I don’t want to lose this meet,” Norm said. His smile was no more inscrutable than ever.

Rather than amusement, it suggested suspicion that he might, after all. be alone in his stated desire, or perhaps amusement at that suspicion, and so on.

“All we have to do is place. Can you place with Hooty?”

“Absolutely,” I said. “Guaranteed.”

“All right,” Norm said. “Get him.”

“I’ll go,” Billy said.

“Now,” Norm said to the two remaining, and now the two fastest, members of the relay team, i. e., Fichter and me. “Order. Who’s anchoring this relay?”

Although Fichter did not deign to reply to this query, and so I said, “I am.”

“What are you trying to do, throw the meet?” Fichter said. “I’m the fastest.”

“Yes, Leo, but you also have much the best flat start,” I said. “True or not true?”

"Well, true," Fichter said, failing to blush.

"And when the other teams see you lead off, they'll assume we have an even faster swimmer than you in reserve to swim last, despite the fact that Chip is out. They'll lose heart. Meanwhile, I move up from third to anchor. Billy swims third, Hooty goes second."

Seeming both pleased and intrigued by this exchange, Norm Cohen looked from me to Fichter and back to me again.

"All right," he said, as Billy brought Hooty up to join us. "Now remember. All you have to do is place. Swim hard. Safe starts."

We would place. As a direct result, our team would win the meet. And, in the event, so to speak—with cheers detonating around us like depth charges and with bodies dropping off the blocks into the water to either side, with Cindy watching alone in the stands and Mr. Hurwitz taking a dazed moment from his duties to cheer for his son, with Fichter watching open-mouthed beside me and Chip maybe staring into an open, empty locker, although I think that was him standing next to Norm—under the circumstances, I did the only thing I could. As Hooty flipped at our feet at the end of the second and antepenultimate length of his leg and pushed off for the third and penultimate length, and as Billy stepped onto the block to take his mark for his leg of the relay, I reached up and grabbed my brother by the wrist. In the midst of the fray of the freestyle relay, he turned to me with the placid, trusting expression I had seen on his face at least once before. Tugging him off the block, in what must have seemed a pantomime to all the aforesaid spectators, I suggested, or advised, or exhorted him to swim the anchor leg and bring home a victory for the team. Then I climbed onto the block in his place. And like my teammates and/or brothers and/or brother, I swam like a banshee.

And Billy brought us home.

CHAPTER TWENTY

Household Order

"You won the meet," Mrs. Livingstone said when Billy failed to arrive.

"I had nothing to do with it," Chip said.

"Teddy did, from what I hear," Mr. Livingstone said.

"Yes, he did," Chip said with a look in his brother's direction. "You might say he was instrumental."

Mr. and Mrs. Livingstone recoiled to the backs of their respective chairs as though on rocket sleds. Their initial reaction to any family crisis was to let all waves of emotional G-force, usually emanating from Chip, wash over them.

.

Since then Chip was standing, and everyone else was stock-still. When the bell rang, he was the one to open the front door onto an unlikely group of carolers. It was the Howard Hurwitzes, Sr. and Jr., and Billy and Cindy, all back from the post-Christmas meet party. From the way they were greeted with cheerful peals of inquiry about that social function, they would naturally have concluded the Livingstones had been having a party of their own.

"Chip, I'm still sick about what happened today," Mr. Hurwitz said, having declined the offer of a drink and/or seat. "I still don't know how it happened, but I take full responsibility."

"Don't worry about it, Howie," Mr. Livingstone said. "Next year you'll know the ropes."

"Next year at this time I'm going to arrange to be at a professional meeting in Australia," Mr. Hurwitz said, "unless I can find one farther away. Billy, you can take it from here."

"Yes sir," Billy answered.

"Then good night, all," Mr. Hurwitz said. "And happy Christmas to you."

After Chip, who had remained at the door like a porter

during this scene, had shown Mr. Hurwitz and Hooty out, Mrs. Livingstone pronounced the single word, "Cindy."

"Cindy was my date to the party," Billy said.

"Oh," Mrs. Livingstone said brightly.

"Yes, it was a nice thought, Teddy," Billy said. "But we decided in the car that, even though Cindy was technically my date, you should drive her home."

Flanking the Christmas tree, lusterless at the moment with its unlit bulbs and its boughs bare of tinsel, Chip and Billy looked at Teddy in unison, as though Billy's decision was indeed a corporate one. All at once they looked very adult to Teddy, and very much like brothers, like two adult brothers, maybe partners in a family law firm.

"There you have it, Dad, motive and opportunity," Chip said, as though subliminally picking up on his youngest brother's legal fantasy.

"Come again?" Mr. Livingstone asked.

"The answers to your objections, Dad. I think Teddy just wanted things back the way they used to be. And he got his wish. Am I right, Teddy? Close?"

Now everyone was looking at Teddy.

"Close," Teddy said.

"It's all just coming to fruition, and into focus," Chip said.

"Billy has a girlfriend again, at least for a day. Although I don't think Teddy orchestrated that. (That was just one lucky break. Teddy doesn't have a girlfriend, precisely because Billy does.)"

"I'm not following you, Chip," Mr. Livingstone said.

"Romantically speaking, then, everything is the way it was. On the other hand, Teddy set a couple of things to right today. Billy finally beat me, if only because I wasn't allowed to compete; and Billy got to anchor a successful relay. I guess Teddy's never forgotten about the second Chapel Gate meet last summer, or forgiven me. Has he?"

"I guess not," Teddy said, his memory suddenly flooded with the sunlight of a late summer afternoon. "You set Billy up to lose that day, the relay and the meet. We would have lost, too, if Progar hadn't false started for Chapel Gate. You should have anchored that relay, Chip. It was your duty as a swimmer and a brother. You're the oldest and the fastest."

"You know, he's probably right," Chip said, turning to Billy. "I've thought back to that moment many times since then. I'm still not sure if I genuinely thought we had a better chance to win the relay if I went third or if I just couldn't stand the thought of trying to beat Progar one more time head-to-head. It's something I just did. I shouldn't have put you in that position. I'm sorry."

"It's okay," Billy said. "It worked out."

"There's still more to Teddy's plan," Chip said, reanimated. "He got his best friend Hooty into the freestyle relay."

"Cindy?" Teddy asked. "Do you remember when you told me that you thought I dragged my injury out last summer so that Hooty would have a chance to swim in the championships?"

Cindy nodded carefully.

"Well, I didn't. At least, I don't recall that I did. Maybe I did. But you made it sound as though I should have. This time I wanted to be sure."

Teddy did not detect in Cindy the flash of enlightenment he'd expected. Only maybe there was a flash of discomfort, further discomfort. No one had as yet sat down.

"Teddy can come and go pretty much as he pleases in the Hurwitz household," Chip said.

"Pretty much," Teddy said.

"But somehow I think there was another reason why he got hold of my entry form and changed the time, and this may be the most important reason. He wanted me to be disappointed—not just to be mean, but so that I would realize that I really did want to compete, that swimming mattered to me. In a way I think Teddy did it for me."

"Teddy?" Mrs. Livingstone asked.

"I don't think people understand how hard it is when you

have to pick who it is you want to love," Teddy said.

As he spoke, he wasn't sure he had ever before so completely had the attention of others, or for that matter of himself.

"I have two brothers, and I would like to be able to love them both equally. But all my life, almost every day, I've had to choose between them, in ways I couldn't even explain. Maybe that is a weakness of mine, or maybe the choice was forced on me. I am sure, though, that I'm not the only one who has chosen. It's obvious Chip is everyone's favorite. But no one ever mentions the obvious. I think maybe I was afraid that we would just go on in the same way forever, out of habit. I suppose I wanted us to be able to start over with it all. I don't know. It's hard."

"Teddy," Mrs. Livingstone said, although it was really someone else's turn to be announced.

The silence that followed was broken unexpectedly.

"I wish you all could see yourselves for just a minute the way I do," Cindy said. "I grew up convinced that my family was the only flawed one in the neighborhood. Every other family seemed so perfectly normal. When they went inside their houses, they didn't scream and yell at each other. They could go out to a restaurant without getting into a fight. I know now that there is no such thing as a happy family. But maybe it would help you to know that you look happy to me, even right now."

"Teddy, will you ask Cindy to dinner?" Mrs. Livingstone asked, "or should I ask Billy to invite her? I can't recall what Emily Post says about this social situation."

Before Teddy could decide this point of etiquette, his father walked across the room toward him, red-faced, his jaw quivering with disapproval bordering on rage. He clamped his hand around Teddy's upper arm.

"Teddy," he said. "Invite this girl to dinner." Then his features relaxed from what proved to be mock disapproval bordering on mock rage as he added, "That's an order!"

Mrs. Livingstone walked over to Cindy, put a hand on each of her shoulders and looked into her eyes.

"That's a joke," she said. "A family joke. We do hope you can stay to dinner. Can you call your parents to see if it's all right with them?"

"We're having spaghetti," Chip said. "Isn't that traditional on the night before Christmas Eve?"

"You can help us put the tinsel on the tree," Billy said. "We'll do it a day early in your honor."

"Just put your presents for us down there with the others," Chip said.

Cindy looked around from one to the other of the Livingstones with a comic pout.

"Thank you," she said. "I'll call. I'll leave a message with the baby sitter if my parents aren't home yet."

"And, Teddy, will you call Mr. Hurwitz afterwards?" Mrs. Livingstone asked. "He must feel awful."

"Yes, Mom, I will," Teddy said.

When the calls had been made, the group sat down at the dining room table where they ate and talked and laughed surprisingly normally.

And After winter there always comes the spring. . .

www.ingramcontent.com/pod-product-compliance
Ingram Content Group UK Ltd.
Pitfield, Milton Keynes, MK11 3LW, UK
UKHW020121200726
13856UKWH00002B/664